The Girl
Pretending
To Read
Rilke

D1568814

The Girl Pretending To Read Rilke

a novel

by

Barbara Riddle

Pilgrim's Lane Press

The Girl Pretending to Read Rilke
a novel by Barbara Riddle
Copyright © 2000, 2013 Barbara Riddle

All rights reserved under International and Pan-American Copyright
conventions.

ISBN: 978-0-615-90432-0 (paperback)

Printed in the United States

First published by Renaissance Sound and Publications, San Francisco,
CA, March 2000.

2013 edition published by Pilgrim's Lane Press

This is a work of fiction. The characters, incidents and dialogues are
products of the author's imagination.

Grateful acknowledgment is made for permission to use the following:

"Evening," by R.M. Rilke, from **RILKE,** Selected Poems. Bilingual
Edition. Translated/edited by C.F. MacIntyre. Copyright (c) 1940, 1968.
University of California Press.

Excerpt:
Letter to Lou Andreas-Salome, quoted on page 207-208 from **LETTERS
TO A YOUNG POET** by Rainer Maria Rilke, translated by M.D. Herter
Norton. Copyright 1934, 1954 by W.W. Norton & Company, Inc., renewed
(c)1962, 1982 by M.D. Herter Norton. Used by permission of W.W. Norton
& Company, Inc.

Front cover design: Michael Atman
(photo of Barbara Riddle supplied by author)
Rear cover design: Richard Zybert Graphics

Pilgrim's Lane Press

Suite 321
701 Mirror Lake Drive N.
St. Petersburg, Fl. 33701

For Laramie

Evening

Slowly now the evening changes his garments
held for him by a rim of ancient trees;
you gaze; and the landscape divides and leaves you,
one sinking and one rising toward the sky.

And you are left, to none belonging wholly,
not so dark as a silent house, nor quite
so surely pledged unto eternity
as that which grows to star and climbs the night.

To you is left (unspeakably confused) - your life,
gigantic, ripening, full of fears,
so that it, now hemmed in, now grasping all,
is changed in you by turns to stone and stars.

Rainer Maria Rilke

Prologue

June, 1963

BRONWEN was ready for love, her legs freshly shaved that morning but already the little prickles forming, it was no use, you could never keep up with your own biology, your blood pumping, all systems go—and then maybe something would remind him of the last girlfriend, the really bright one, and you'd just have to survive that lull, that little pause in the rhythm of desire that you detect when you're the one who's really in love. And was she? Bronwen looked out the window as Boston took shape in the cold blue dawn. Soon the plane would land, she'd be in a cab and then in Eric's bed. Her unread *New Republic* slid off her lap onto the floor. Her brain was unprepared but oh her body was ready. The bad, bad daughter flying directly from college to her summer job and boyfriend's bed, skipping the depressing visit home and her father's litany of all things wrong with America. She liked her life, let him go to a bar and chew the ear off some bartender, nobody was going to make her feel guilty about not going home first. Home? A rented studio apartment in Pasadena with a bunch of sun-spotted loonies in much too revealing bathing suits showing each other their surgical scars. Ugh. The FASTEN SEAT BELTS light flashed on. She smiled. Hormones keened brightly in her blood, and her eyesight dimmed with lust. It was not a bad thing, not bad at all, to have finished her junior year at a tough college, to have a paying summer job at one of the best biochem labs on the East Coast, and to have a Harvard Junior Fellow awaiting her arrival. It wasn't his fault if he was too busy to meet her at the airport.

Maybe she should at least skim the copy of I.F. Stone's Weekly that was crammed into her shoulder bag. There was still time, while they circled over the landing area. Eric might ask, indirectly maybe, but he'd probe her brain, tongue it like a rotten tooth. He wanted her to be up on things when they mingled with his friends. CIA Cover-Up! Troop Build-ups Just The Beginning! Exclusive interview inside.

It was all starting to come back. The sensation of being watched, and judged. And found wanting. She would never be smart enough.

Now the stewardesses were strolling past, in high heels, picking up paper cups half-full of ginger ale and tossing them in plastic garbage bags. Their make-up was perfect, their legs inhumanly smooth. How did they keep their hair turned under like that, flawless blonde curtains of hair flowing over their navy blue shoulders, not a fleck of dandruff in sight. They clustered in back, buckling themselves down for the descent. The pitch of their laughter indicated to Bronwen that their thoughts were not far from her own. Perhaps the tall pilot with the clipped silver mustache would be meeting one of them...

She glanced down at her sandals and jeans. Who'd ever guess that a passionate siren lurked beneath? But all that was at least two hours ahead. Grumpily, she smoothed out the newsletter in her lap. Crisp sentences entered her consciousness and immediately crumbled into a dust of scattered facts. It was hopeless. Her mind skittered from headline to headline and then off the page completely. Today there was only one reality, and all her neurons were dumb with anticipation.

Indeed, the concept of mind no longer applied to Bronwen for this brief interlude. She had become, in effect, a single humongous nerve cell.

* * * *

Chapter 1

IT WAS the fourth night in a row that Paulette had turned away from him. Felix couldn't help it, coming home at 3 or 4 a.m. after wrapping up a successful experiment, he wanted to celebrate, to make love to the universe. And sweet Paulette was Felix's own private slice of perfection, the nearest vessel for transfer of the joy that was pumping through his veins.

Felix gazed at her sleeping form. He knew that gossip around the lab had it that she was smarter than he, that although of near genius I.Q. her plain face had made her all too willing to accept the proposal from a bum such as himself. But this year he would definitely finish the doctorate, it was only a matter of the last two chapters and he already had rough drafts of those. He was well aware that his appointment to the junior teaching faculty at Harvard was conditional upon completing his requirements within the year and he *would* meet that deadline.

He smirked in the dark as he thought how badly they must have wanted him to have made that exception in the first place, taking him without the formal degree.

The only wild card was the possibility that Professor Couveau might want him to repeat that series that gave them some unexpected results when he had been rushing to finish up last year.

As he worried, he twisted Paulette's long frizzy blonde curls around his pinky. Her hair was spread loosely over the pillow, freed from its usual confining brown metal barrette, worn low on the back of her neck like a schoolgirl's. She was immediately recognizable at a great distance down the hall, gliding along in her crepe-soled sandals with a rack of test tubes balanced carefully in her hands. She had perfect, slender legs, with just the hint of a tan acquired during the week they'd spent at her parents' house on the Maine coast. From their nervousness, he guessed he was probably the first Jew to spend an entire night, not to mention seven, under their roof.

He lifted her upper lip with the forefinger of his free hand, to peek at the little gap between her front teeth. She groaned and turned her head away. It was truly hopeless tonight. He'd stop pestering her.

Felix glanced at the clock radio, set by her for the usual 7:30. Damn it all. Tomorrow the new summer research assistant—weird name, Olwen, Bronwen, something Celtic and please not an old-money debutante—would show up at nine sharp, and it was 3:30 already. His eyelids drooped as he tucked his knees behind the shapely ones of his wife. The old image was taking form again, the one where Paulette was gazing adoringly up at him from below the podium as he accepted the Prize, the big N, for his devastatingly seminal work on the basic biology of bacterial viruses. He looked svelte and sophisticated in his black tie and tails, having dropped 30 pounds before embarking for Stockholm.

Sweden ... Denmark ... Danish pastries at the buffet afterwards ... If he remembered correctly, there was one only slightly stale jelly doughnut left over from yesterday somewhere in the kitchen. Felix extricated himself from the warmth of his marriage bed and lurched naked down the hall of their Cambridge flat, leaning way over on the balls of his feet, his soft belly plopping gently in the dark as he hurried towards his goal.

Chapter 2

OF all the many names Felix had been called in his life, philanderer was not among them. When Bronwen knocked timidly on the open door of his office that morning, he looked up from his desk and barely registered the fact that she was female. Like wild geese, he and Paulette were mated for life and he responded to other humans mainly in terms of how quickly they appreciated his quirky wit and not inconsiderable intelligence.

"So. You say you're a chemistry major, but mainly interested in genetics?"

He wiggled around in his swivel chair, tapping his empty meerschaum pipe nervously on the stack of rough thesis drafts that cluttered his desk and spilled onto the floor. "Why?" He stopped jiggling around to stare directly into her, as he now noticed, pale blue eyes. She was about nineteen years old, he guessed.

Trying not to let her eyes focus on the safety pin protruding from the hinge on the left side of Felix's glasses, Bronwen attempted to return his gaze. To control her impulse to laugh, she frowned and looked down at her feet. They were unappealingly white in contrast to the dark leather of her old sandals. Would there be any time to get a tan this summer?

She looked up again. "Well, genetics because of the mystery. Chemistry because it's a necessary evil en route to answering the most interesting questions. A bit boring a lot of the time, granted, but it'll get me where I want to go. Understanding how one fertilized egg turns into a brain, and feet ... and eyeballs ..." She was now composed enough to look right into his eyes, kind of googly behind his thick lenses. He was much younger than she had expected, and seemed to be kind of hyper.

"Excuse me, ah," he looked down at a file folder in front of him, "Bronwen, that theoretical stuff is all well and good, but our kind of science is done by real people doing real experiments. Are you going to be willing to stay nights, things like that? How late did you plan to stay today, for example? This isn't a nine-to-five kind of operation we're running, you know."

Cheeks flushing, Bronwen summoned all her will power to maintain eye contact with him. "I realize that. I can stay until 11 if necessary. The last train for Cambridge leaves at 11:14. I don't have a car. But I intend to make good use of my time in your laboratory and I am grateful for the chance I've been given." It was going to be even worse than everyone said

Felix grunted. This summer's intern might be a little more promising than last year's, who had been more concerned with improving his tennis serve than learning assay techniques. At least she hadn't said anything about fame and fortune, or curing cancer in the next two months. He might have a colleague here after all. Bronwen could possibly help him repeat some of those troublesome experiments so he could wrap up his degree and get Paulette and the Department off his case.

Rising from his chair in one abrupt movement, he paused, rocking back and forth on the balls of his feet, the usual early morning sweat stains beginning to darken his armpits. He couldn't remember if he had used Paulette's deodorant or not. She had taken to hiding it from him. He pulled absentmindedly at his underpants, girding his loins for the day ahead.

"All right, let's get you started. First, a clean lab coat."

Felix careened down the hall, sticking his head into every doorway they passed, with Bronwen following close behind. She almost crashed into him twice.

"Aha! Inge won't mind if we borrow one of hers. She's on a kind of ... unofficial leave of absence." He snatched a long, starchy coat off a hook on the back of a door marked "Dr. Bergenstrasser" and tossed the garment to Bronwen. She slipped it on over her olive cotton tank top and khaki bermudas. It hung far past her knees and the sleeves hid her hands completely. Inge must be a Valkyrie. She rolled up the sleeves and buttoned up the front. Her brain felt as stiff and white as the coat. There was a hot tingly sensation under her eyes and at the tip of her nose, like the onset of homesickness on the first day of summer camp.

Felix surveyed her. "Perfect! Come, my little chickadee, and I'll show you how we wash our pipettes." His W.C. Fields imitation went right over her head, he realized, and he resolved to tone himself down, at least for the first few days.

He was pure business as he showed her how to delicately lift the rack of pipettes out of the caustic bath of permanganate acid that would dissolve and destroy any contaminants. Then the thin glass tubes would be hooked to an overnight rinsing mechanism and doused with distilled water, dried in an autoclave and finally stored neatly according to size in large drawers, like kitchen silverware. The warm, clean pipettes would squeak under your fingers if done right, he claimed. As he said this, he saw his mother by a window in a patch of sun, toweling her wet hair dry, showing his father how it squeaked when she pulled it tight. The whiffs of acidic air that escaped when he took the cover off the pipette rack were bizarrely familiar, distant cousin to that sour-sweet smell of the cider vinegar hair rinse that his mother used to let him pour over her long chestnut hair as she kneeled by the bathtub with her head lost in the heavy, wet mass she was so proud of. Felix started another speech meant to impress upon Bronwen that working with viruses was very different from doing a mere chemistry experiment; any trace of biological contamination could ruin weeks or months of results—even waste *years* of a researcher's life. He cut himself short from extolling the virtues of correctly performing this lowly task when he saw that she gave no sign of resenting it, no sign of any emotion but eagerness to please, to do everything perfectly.

He himself never bothered with lab coats, and his shirts and pants were peppered with little holes where he had dribbled the cloth-eating acid. It was almost the only habit Paulette nagged him about, but he just couldn't be bothered. He'd been a bachelor for too long. It was hard enough giving up the pipe. He still carried the soft plastic pouch in his pocket, filled with the cheap artificial-rum-soaked tobacco mixture that Paulette had once found so appealing.

Bronwen shakily lowered the heavy rack of pipettes into the vat of thick garnet-colored liquid that actually bubbled and gurgled as the rack settled in and acid forced the air out of the glass rods. The skin on her hands smarted from their brief exposure to the fumes wafting from this witches' brew. Such a crude substance, but science wouldn't be possible without it. She felt slightly dizzy from holding her breath, trying to avoid breathing while she was close to it.

Now Felix was handing her some reprints and asking her to read them, then help him set up an experiment this afternoon. Bronwen accepted them gratefully and set off down the hall. Success! She had survived her first encounter with the infamous Felix—without shedding a single tear.

Felix was totally exhausted. Maybe he could sneak in a nap out in the parking lot after lunch. He just wasn't used to coming in this early. It seemed that this mentoring business was not all that glamorous when you came right down to it.

"*You're very late.*" Eric was grumpy. He'd been sleeping.

"I know, sorry. I really didn't have a chance to call. He's kind of a madman, you were right. Were you worried? He insisted on giving me a ride home. I think he was kind of ashamed that we wound up working so late on my first day." Bronwen dropped her underpants to the floor and slid under the sheet, moving closer to Eric's side of the bed.

"Why would I worry? Just need to sleep, that's all, giving a talk tomorrow and I have to get up early." He turned over after patting her shoulder once. Within seconds he was snoring lightly.

Not tired at all, she sighed and picked up her copy of "The Collected Poems of Rainer Maria Rilke." This summer she would read everything by Rilke she could find. She had decided to "specialize" in Rilke. All the scientists in Eric's crowd had a little niche, a subarea of nontechnical knowledge on which they could hold forth. There were Red China-watchers, and chamber music freaks, motorcycle connoisseurs—you name it. Poetry was not especially popular.

"You're very late." Paulette was grumpy. She'd been sleeping. She'd expected him for dinner. The veal roast was all dried out, the dinner rolls burned and the very expensive asparagus a stringy mess. She'd left it all on the kitchen counter to shame him. What made her really mad was that she'd eaten half of the home-made strawberry shortcake herself.

"It's our anniversary." Her back was a hump under the sheet, her voice muffled. Her new policy was not to remind him of anything. His mother had always taken care of the annoying little daily details for him but she wasn't going to do it.

"Lettie-bunch, I knew that, but I was in the library finishing the last draft of Chapter 10." It was a white lie for a good cause. "The end is nigh! Lettie?" Silence. "And to celebrate, I'm taking you to Chez Adrienne tomorrow night! I already have reservations!" Still no response. He lifted the Marimekko sheet (wedding present from her parents) and, murmuring in her ear, in his best Mae West contralto, "Do you mind if I slip into something more comfortable?" he put his hand between her legs and let it linger there until she turned to him, the weight of him, the whole infuriating phenomenon of Felix.

Chapter 3

BRONWEN followed Eric cautiously through the narrow doorway of Eric's favorite Army surplus store. They had enough money to pay for two pairs of white Levi's, in honor of summer, and hamburgers at Sammy's Deli on the Square afterwards. Maybe there'd even be enough for Sam's Famous Onion Rings. It was the first free time she'd had since arriving and meeting Felix, who had turned out to be both less intimidating and more goofy than she had expected.

The interior of the store was cool and dim. Eyes adjusting to the darkness, they made their way down the long aisles, inhaling the familiar smells of slightly moldy canvas duffel bags and new cotton. Piles of brightly colored t-shirts were stacked on every available surface.

As usual, Eric picked his pair right off the shelf and went directly to the cash register while she went towards the changing area. She was aware of him flipping impatiently through his *New York Times* while he waited for her to emerge from behind the white sheet that formed the curtain for the dressing cubicle. His friend Harvey had written a Letter to the Editor about U.S. policy in Southeast Asia and there was going to be a big discussion at lunch. She would be mostly silent, slurping the last drops of her coffee malted through a straw, and licking the delicious salty grease from the onion rings off her fingertips, waiting until she and Eric could be alone.

Bronwen knew that Eric was in a hurry to join the others, but she didn't dare buy jeans without trying them on now that she had started taking the Pill again. You could count on at least a five-pound gain every summer when they resumed living together after the bleak interruption of the academic year. There was no point in spending the money to protect herself during the winter; since Eric had graduated two years ago, no one had even tempted her to be unfaithful. Anyway, with all those chemistry labs, who had time for sex?

She came out and assessed herself uncertainly in the blotchy full length mirror, lit by one bare overhead bulb. The fit in the hips and length was fine, but the waist was inches too big and there was a draft at the small of her back where the material gaped open, just under the blunt-cut ends of her thick brown hair.

Her thighs seemed much wider in white than in blue denim. Still, this was summer and this was the garment of choice in Boston. Next week, after getting her first paycheck, she'd come back for one of those genuine—even to the sweat stains—blue and white striped sailor's jerseys.

"They're fine. Let's *go*. Harvey's meeting us at 12:30." She glanced over, but his eyes had reverted back to the Editorial page. His lips moved ever so slightly as he read, and from this distance he looked about fourteen. The 3-inch difference in their heights had never bothered her; if anything, it made him somewhat exotic. And, of course, his intensity more than compensated. With his Napoleonic swagger and his cropped Bertolt Brecht bangs cut high on his forehead, he often caused stares when he dismounted from his twin cylinder BMW motorcycle in front of the staid Harvard Biological Laboratory. She had watched more than one security guard regret asking this arrogant young graduate student for his University I.D. card late at night, only to be informed that he was impeding the progress of medical science and would be reported if he caused any further delays by asking ridiculously officious and unnecessary questions.

Bronwen found herself becoming mildly aroused as she thought of Eric running up the steps towards his waiting experiment, his watery hazel eyes glistening behind his tortoise shell glasses, brain click-clicking with hypotheses

Barbara Riddle

and flashes of intuition not even articulated yet. He was brilliant. Everyone said so. And he was her lover.

She decided to wear the new jeans to lunch, recklessly risking ketchup stains. Perhaps they would have time to go back to their apartment and make love before Eric went to work. This was probably the last free day she'd have for weeks. Rumor had it that Felix liked to harass his research assistants until they broke down and begged for time off. She was going to surprise him.

Bronwen and Eric each presented the clerk with a ten dollar bill, and each carefully collected their respective two dollars and change.

He walked behind her, smacking her ass appreciatively with the folded newspaper. "Not bad, Fishface, not bad at all. What say we go back and Do It after lunch?" He jerked the bike off its kickstand and mounted it. After several aggressive kicks, the engine roared to life.

Bronwen climbed on, careful to keep her right calf away from the exhaust pipe. There was an ugly three-inch long burn mark left over from last year, and one scar was enough. Her knees hugged his thighs and they were off, helmetless, the paper bag with their clothes in it jammed securely between her stomach and his back. Summer had officially begun.

Chapter 4

"SO, no fooling now, don't kid a kidder—what really made you go into science?" Felix and Bronwen were in the subsidized university cafeteria, Felix wallowing in his usual Hamburger Special.

"Made me?" Bronwen dipped a french fry into the hill of ketchup on her plate, took a dainty bite, dipped again. After one week of working with the Grizzly (as she now thought of him), she was beginning to enjoy his good-natured bluntness, especially his look of delight when she not only got his jokes but gave him back as good. She challenged herself to see how many times a day she could make him laugh out loud, a generous belly laugh that showed no restraint—or envy that he hadn't made the remark himself. She couldn't recall the last time that had happened with Eric—humor was supposed to be his sacred turf.

"C'mon, don't play coy, you know what I mean, your inspiration. Girls don't just whimsically decide to give up a social life and nice clothes to hang around in smelly hellholes with slavedrivers like me ordering them around..."

Having polished off his burger, fries and coleslaw, he tackled the German chocolate cake with the coconut frosting. "Is that all you're having?" He gestured towards her remaining three fries.

"I never eat much at lunchtime," she lied. She was waiting for her first paycheck, which she would get this afternoon. She was ravenous. "Okay. There was a Mr. Katz..."

"I knew it! Jews everywhere you look! Imparting knowledge to children!"

"... who wore these amazingly white coats to class, and striped ties, and he had very straight teeth and he smiled a lot. And he showed us this movie about plastics, yes, it was called something like "Better Living Through Chemistry," with pictures of all these brightly colored solutions flowing together, and this deep voiceover saying, "Man can create substances that never before existed on this earth—science and man together in a partnership that knows no bounds..." Something like that. It gave me the goosebumps in the dark. I guess it was like being in a church, and it seemed as if scientists could play God and make anything possible."

"And of course it didn't hurt that he looked good in white..."

"Absolutely. I was crushed when he announced to us that he was the proud new father of a baby named Andy. I guess I thought he was going to wait for me to graduate from high school or something. I was about 12, I think. I suppose if he had been my French teacher I would be in a cafe on the Left Bank right now, writing poetry or reading Simone de Beauvoir."

"In which case," said Felix, "your pommes frites would have been far superior." Silence. Bronwen regretted having talked so much. At least she didn't mention falling in love with heroic researcher Martin Arrowsmith when she read the book of that title at fourteen. She must have sounded childish enough already. The image of Martin's wife helping him in the lab, her missing button carelessly replaced by a huge safety pin, flitted across her mind and she smiled involuntarily. She would be like that, oblivious and dedicated to mankind. Maybe someday she and Eric would work together, eating peanut-butter sandwiches late into the night.

For the moment, she was desperately hungry. She pushed her fist into her stomach to keep it from growling too loudly in the growing silence.

Felix was being very quiet, for Felix. His mind was a chaos of sarcastic one-liners that he kept rejecting as fast as they occurred to him. He wasn't used to such a hypersensitive audience. Here was a person who actually listened to what he said. Her smile encouraged him to continue. He tried to recapture the mood. "Really, Bronwen, you don't think it was that random, do you? There was something that you ...that I also felt at that age, yes? A need for something to make sense, for the world to be pure and logical. To give yourself to something that would always be...reliable. Constant. And yet full of surprises. Daily. Impossible to resist."

Her face was a polite blank. In truth, she had an urgent need to pee.

Felix flailed forward. "Don't you still feel that way? About science, that is? Passionate .... Even if you'd never met your Mr. Katz ..." She had closed herself off. Damn. He realized he was rambling and checked the large wall clock above the steam table. It was 2:20! They were the only patrons remaining in the room.

Margaret, the thin, elderly Irish server in a black hairnet that imprisoned her wisps of dull reddish-brown hair, white at the roots, banged around pointedly behind them. When they left, she would be done for the day.

She began washing the stainless steel food bins with scalding water from a hose that she aimed expertly as she hobbled along the wooden pallets that formed a walkway on the inside of the lunch counter. There was no sound except the splat and whoosh of water against metal.

"Our friendly neighborhood bacteria should be ready to harvest by 2:45." Felix's voice was soft and restrained. "We'd better go back and do the cell count to see if they're ready, yes?"

He pushed himself from the table and Bronwen followed. Shoving open the lunchroom's double doors, they hit the searing heat of midday and walked slowly side by side up the asphalt path to the Ethel and Morris Singer Memorial biochemistry building, entering from the back, past huge receptacles labeled DANGER: RADIOACTIVE WASTE. They gasped simultaneously as the cool air of the hallway enclosed them. She was close enough to inhale the smell of his sweat and was surprised to find it not unpleasant. Felix was so *there* all the time. Eric was never anywhere you wanted him to be.

"You go on up, Bronzie... I'm going to stop by the library and cheer up my wife. She's trying to finish up her damn grant application today. Can you check on our bugs without me? I won't be more than five minutes."

"Of course. See you when you come." She continued down the hall, not sure if she liked the nickname Felix had just invented for her. Sometimes it was hard to tell the difference between being treated like one of the guys or being patronized, but at lunch she felt like an invisible line had been crossed. Felix was starting to treat her like someone with a future.

She spotted a Ladies' Room and sprinted towards the blessed door. This was her last chance to pee before getting ensnared for the next two hours.

The cheap aluminum mirror inside reflected a pale, purple-tinged face, every mosquito bite emphasized by the unflattering light. The blue and green striped t-shirt was not helping. Her breasts, not yet swollen by the Pill, were virtually hidden in the loose folds of cotton. With her hair pulled back, her ears were more prominent than ever. A good thing looks weren't a prerequisite for the job. She couldn't imagine working as a waitress, having to look sharp for 10 hours at a stretch. But then, she couldn't imagine doing anything but what she was doing. Honestly, she would have paid *them* to let her do it if she didn't have the research fellowship. It was strange that she happened to be here, and not someone else. What if she was just wasting everyone's money?

She hurried out after carefully washing her hands. (Musn't give germs to the germs.) The pleasant lunchtime mood was rapidly evaporating. Must remember that fluorescent lighting never failed to make her look like the evil twin of Emily Dickinson, and always made her morbid. If she was lucky, there was still half a stale Hershey Bar in her desk drawer.

* * * *

Felix coughed softly. He probably shouldn't have come.

Paulette had that orphaned Cocker Spaniel look again, gazing up at him from the chaos of journals, index cards and scribbled legal pads that would somehow congeal into a finished grant application by midnight tomorrow. She'd work all night, then bring it sweetly to the departmental secretary at 8:30 a.m., along with a box of her homemade walnut fudge. There was always a perfect draft back on Paulette's desk by 5 p.m. Even the fudge wasn't strictly necessary. Everyone liked Paulette; she was every secretary's dream boss. Felix knew they *hated* it when his grant renewal time came up, they knew he'd be running in and out all week, thrusting revised pages at them, asking them to go back, insert, renumber, cut and paste, add a paragraph in the middle of page eight. He couldn't help it. It wasn't as if he was trying to be obnoxious. He just didn't know how other people did it: up at 7:30, coffee, The Globe, out by 8:15, start the cultures growing, line up the glassware, weigh the substrates on the microbalance, ready to start by 9:30 latest. Most mornings,

Felix would still be in bed, wrestling with the sheets, wondering if he'd locked up the lab when he left at midnight, hoping he had one clean shirt in his closet. Paulette would be long gone, only a trace of her green, woodsy cologne in the air, her scuffed black leather ballet slippers in a heap under the kitchen table. Looking at her things, he would be flooded with love for the quick sharp way she threaded herself through her life, one neat stitch at a time.

He smiled at her now, prisoner of the science library, and stage-whispered, "Did you eat?" She answered with a brief, tight smile of her own, pointing dramatically to her pile of papers and then down to her lunch bag on the floor. "Later."

She hunched back over her clipboard and continued scribbling. Felix took the hint and ambled out of the room, but her eyes had pierced his soul. He felt transparent as an x-ray. Insubstantial, light-headed. She was beginning to lose faith in him, he could feel it. This summer might be his last chance to save his job, his reputation and his marriage. He scrunched up his forehead as he quickly calculated that several times they had gone for 10 days or more without making love.

At that instant Felix decided he would take a week off, fly to Canada and have the marathon session Couveau had been pleading for. Bronwen could muddle along somehow, his section would continue to appear productive in his absence and perhaps having a novice get the same results he had gotten last year would be further ammunition for his hypothesis. He'd give her a week's worth of protocols to follow, and he'd come back to crisp new data and a loving wife. Yes! Better living through chemistry, indeed.

Felix swung recklessly into the lab, narrowly missing the cart bearing a huge glass carboy containing 50 gallons of a cloudy bacterial culture in the full throes of doubling its population every 15 minutes.

This behemoth always looked to Felix like an enormous vase of eggdrop soup. Bronwen was gingerly guiding the stainless steel cart around the sink, being careful to avoid snagging its corners on any of the many lengths of tubing that dangled from various countertops and faucets. For a second, Felix had a flash of a woman in a supermarket, comparison shopping for brands of peanut butter and breakfast cereal, telling him to be quiet or she wouldn't buy the brand with the little plastic zoo animals. Women were always telling you to be quiet, to be polite, to be good. He resisted the temptation to run in the opposite direction.

"They're ready?" His redundant question hung stupidly in the air.

"Yup. Just this minute. I took a reading. And the protocol's on your desk. You want to check it? I added a couple of controls, based on that article you gave me to read yesterday. Could you make sure I picked the right concentrations to test?"

Felix was pleased but somehow pissed off, too. Where did everyone else get their energy? And it seemed that Bronwen was kind of smirking as she walked away. He turned around and saw her white Keds disappear out the door. He sat down to read what she had put together, but he was suddenly very tired. The heavy lunch was clumping in his brain and stomach. He wanted to be at home, in bed with Paulette, watching the muslin curtains move in and out with the breeze while she slept with her head resting on his broad, smooth chest.

Chapter 5

FELIX could see Paulette's mouth moving, and he knew she was talking, but he couldn't hear the words. He understood she was angry. He watched her slicing the mushrooms for the salad, holding a firm gray button with her left hand, briskly working her way from right to left with the little French knife, creating a tidy pile of miniature atomic cloud silhouettes. He was late. Again. That was nothing so unusual. But Paulette's eyes were so cold and dull. *That* was unusual. He felt the chill all over his body. Now she was mincing the warm bacon, with quick motions that made him nauseous.

Felix made a mental note: no spinach salad this winter when his parents came up from Florida to visit their finally-married son. He could hardly imagine his mother's face were they to present her with raw mushrooms *and* bacon in the same dish at the same time and place. Come to think of it, maybe he could get Ma to teach Paulette how to make her spinach borscht with the boiled potatoes, and on top, a dollop of sour cream with a spritz of fresh dill. That would keep Ma busy and off his back.

Paulette tilted the cutting board over the teak salad bowl and the expensive morsels of gray fungi slid towards the warm garlic-scented marinade. It was a rare evening alone at home, but the charged atmosphere in the kitchen was beginning to give Felix a sharp pain in the side. Even the comforting odors of rosemary and olive oil wafting from the oven where a Cornish game hen was meeting its maker did not compensate for the frown lines that marred Paulette's usually placid brow.

Through his fog of anxiety, her words slowly became audible. "And I'm not sure, not at all, but you know that I'm never late, although I have been under a lot of pressure working on the grant proposal, but it's just the timing...the timing isn't what we had talked about at all. And if your position isn't renewed..." She was viciously dissecting a carrot into round cross-sections, not looking up as she spoke, the nape of her neck covered, as usual, by her thick streaked blonde hair caught in the ubiquitous brown metal barrette.

Gradually the content of her words began to impinge on Felix's consciousness. A surge of adrenalin flooded his brain and his empty stomach betrayed him. His knees gave way and he began to fall, but as he keeled over he reached out to the table for support. In one grand gesture he took the batik tablecloth, brass candlesticks, blue Mexican goblets and the heavy bowl of quietly marinating mushrooms with him.

Paulette loomed above him, pitiless, shouting. "No, I won't let you cop out this time. This isn't funny!" But she was laughing and crying at the same time. Felix lay flat on his back, stunned, with wine vinegar staining his best oxford-cloth shirt and mushrooms dribbling off his hair onto the kitchen linoleum. Gasping, he burbled something about how terrific it was that she might be pregnant, and they should find out for sure, and in the meantime didn't she need to sit down and he would finish cooking. Then her head grew larger and larger, she was kneeling beside him and it was the first time in weeks that they were both fully awake and touching each other. A son! They might have a son! And Felix would be... a father. Father, father, father. It was a dim outline, somebody to the left and just behind the mother.

He stroked Paulette's hair, and kissed her wet cheeks. He would get organized. A father had to be organized, you had to get life insurance and stuff. They lay on the warm, wet kitchen floor listening to the notes of their neighbor's recording of the Goldberg Variations float in through the open window. Exquisite filigrees of Bach laced the humid summer air, cathedrals of lacy sound rose and fell. Could you fucking believe that Glenn Gould? Plenty of time to practice, probably, no kids, no wife. Maybe they'd name the kid Glenn. Or Glenda. Yech. Well, plenty of time for that. First, they had a very important date with a small, overpriced chicken and a quart of Harvard Square's best vanilla ice cream.

And maybe after the baby came he would take piano lessons again. He could practice when he was home babysitting.

His mother would like that. She would really like that a lot.

Chapter 6

IT PROMISED to be a very disappointing afternoon. The shoes of Caesar Baldessori were not just shiny, but pointy. Not a good sign.

But Bronwen was willing to suspend judgment, at least until the seminar was over. It was her almost universally proven theory that there was an inverse relationship between the quality of a scientist's work and that of his shoes: shiny, with tassels, was a very bad omen. Well-buffed black wingtips could merely signify a habit acquired from a banker-father; it might, however, portend a much-scorned pharmaceutical career in the offing: graveyard for failed academics. Beat-up tan desert boots boded well; no socks could signal the imminent announcement of a major breakthrough.

The rating system broke down completely, however, when it came to females: there were so few that almost all the ones who came to speak were outstanding. The terribly clever clumsy ones lived with their mothers, wore brown Oxfords with laces and very thick crepe soles, and no one judged or cared; the sexy ones proved they had a body as well as a mind by wearing heels and tight sweaters, and were the targets of the most aggressive questioning. They invariably turned out to be the smartest and gutsiest, having long since stopped worrying what other people thought of them. They scared everyone, male and female alike, had long affairs with colleagues on the other side of whatever continent they happened to occupy, stayed unmarried and were despised by the wives of the staff members who were brave enough to invite them home for dinner after their presentations.

Most confusing of all were the seemingly-plain closet beauties who hid their long hair under their starched lab coats and wore the above-mentioned ugly, practical shoes; they were beyond attack—too remote to seduce, too infuriating to ignore. Just bright enough, they didn't believe the praise when they got it (he probably just wants to get me into bed) and they were bitter when overt passes were indeed made (he definitely just wants to get me into bed). They were the loneliest of all until they eventually married a soulmate, had two beautiful children, and as career and family thrived, forgot completely about appearances. Their hips widened, they took to wearing embroidered peasant blouses under their white coats and their hair in one thick, gray-streaked braid down the middle of their backs. They became the mainstay of any research group they became part of—mentor, mother-figure, earth goddess. They became better-looking as they aged and mellowed, growing sweet crinkly crow's feet around their eyes and laughing a lot. One of Bronwen's biology professors was such a one, and she would count herself lucky if that was what the Fates had in store for her.

Dr. Baldessori was clearing his throat for silence. Bronwen looked up from her *New Republic* and was electrified to discover that he had hair, actual reddish-gold curly chest hair, peeping out over the collar of his expensive-looking silk shirt. Her eyes opened wider and she jammed the magazine in her satchel.

"Ladies and Gentlemints," he began, flashing the most beautiful teeth she had ever seen. An immaculate, tapering hand covered with the same reddish hair waved a stick of chalk in the air as he turned to face the blackboard. She sat up in her uncomfortable folding chair, one hundred per cent alert. This might be more interesting than she had expected.

Chapter 7

EVERYONE else in Eric's crowd had seen *Casablanca* at least five times. This was the first for Bronwen. She let herself be visually seduced by the glowing black and white images, the silken coils of Ingrid Bergman's perfect pageboy. Bronwen tried to forget she'd ever seen that postcard of Humphrey Bogart on the set, wooden orange crates strapped to his feet to give him the extra ten inches of height he needed to bend over and kiss Ingrid. It was hard to focus on the dialogue when Eric and Harvey and the rest were lip-synching along with the film, in-between munching popcorn and Junior Mints. The lights came up as Rick and the Inspector strolled across the rain-shiny tarmac of the airport, Ingrid and her man winging away over their heads.

"Fantastic, the best." Eric was already in the aisle. "Bronwen! Move it! We're all going over to Harvey's!"

She bumped her way across the knees of people still sitting and holding hands, drawing out the magic of the last scene as long as they could, in no hurry to rush out of the air-conditioned moviehouse into the sticky summer evening. Since Eric knew it by heart, he of course was on to the next event on the agenda. It was always like this. She would always be 4 years or 4 steps behind him. Only in bed were they ever in the same time and place for a few minutes. She didn't even know anymore if she really enjoyed their lovemaking, or if she simply felt a triumph in getting him to acknowledge her existence, to need something from her for a brief interlude in his life. Not that he was any worse than any of the other males in their social group. At least he made her laugh. And there was something else. She called it being in love with him, but really she didn't know what it was. It just kept her coming back to share summers with him, the undergraduate still tagging after the boyfriend who had long since graduated and was destined for very big things.

Right now their destination was Harvey's flat, lair of economics journals and erotic Japanese woodcuts and more stories of Harvey's failures to procure dates with Radcliffe freshmen. Oh well.

Bronwen climbed on the BMW, wrapping her arms around Eric's small, lean frame, pressing her thighs against his. This was the best part of their relationship, Eric looking like some Mad magazine version of Marlon Brando crossed with Napoleon, Bronwen a pale almost-preppie with wind-snarled hair. She was definitely not going to get a tan this summer, not with Felix keeping her such late hours at the lab. Things were going better than she'd expected, anyway. He didn't patronize her and she loved it that she wasn't treated like a 9-to-5 employee. She was doing genuine research! This was one way she could decide to spend her life, if she wanted. Felix wasn't at the cutting edge of biology, like Eric prided himself on being, but the work was solid and necessary. The backdrop for the glitzy stuff. She could function on this level. She didn't have to be a star to be happy. Well, of course, she could still aim for stardom...

With a skid, they braked to a stop and pulled up in front of the two-story wooden frame building that housed Harvey. Eric had a silly look on his face. "Something special may happen tonight. A friend of Harvey works for this psychology grad instructor who's studying psychogenic mushrooms." He wiggled his eyebrows meaningfully.

Bronwen trudged up the two flights to the top floor flat. The door was open. Dan and Sybil were already there, Harvey naturally, and Tom and Muffie. There was a jug of the cheapest supermarket red wine on an old trunk that served as a coffee table, and people were sitting on cushions on the floor or in one of the two black canvas butterfly chairs that were Harvey's prize possessions. Harvey himself took up most of the sagging maroon alpaca couch that he had rescued from the sidewalk last summer. He was clutching a 7-Up and leering at everyone who entered. Bronwen avoided the empty space next to him on the couch, knowing full well the effect of its prickly upholstery on a warm night and also to avoid the touch of his wandering hands on her exposed kneecaps. Thank goodness she was wearing her Bermudas, so she could sit cross-legged on the floor and not worry about her crotch.

She looked around. The others undoubtedly had their minds on more lofty subjects. Or, perhaps not. Eric flung himself down next to Harvey, but she knew that he had already scanned every woman in the room and could tell you who was wearing a bra and panties, and who wasn't. Sybil fell emphatically in the "wasn't" category. Bronwen was pretty sure that Eric and the high-cheekboned Sybil had been sleeping together last winter, but she didn't ask and hadn't been told. Somehow she'd get through this evening. God, what a long week it had been. Tomorrow was Saturday, at last. But was she supposed to go to the lab? And when was Felix going to Canada? She wouldn't mind a respite from the pace he'd set.

And what was the deal with that Caesar Baldessori today? It was hard to know whether there was anything genuine about him. Although, if truth be told, there was no question that he was the sexiest biochemist she had yet encountered in her admittedly brief career. It wasn't fair to judge him too harshly just because of his looks. Maybe she'd take a shot at testing one of his ideas in the system she and Felix were studying.

Her eyelids drooped, and she let her body slump against the wall near the doorway to the kitchen. There was a strong ammonia scent wafting from the unchanged kitty litter. Harvey was finally telling them that in one week he was going to supply each of them with a peyote button and the use of his flat for the weekend, and they were going to inaugurate a new chapter in the history of Cambridge, Massachusetts.

Chapter 8

IT WAS clear to Bronwen that this wasn't how Harvey had imagined it would be, not at all. He was lying on his back, concentrating all his brainpower on preventing the ceiling from slowly lowering itself down onto him. There were the snakes in the corner, too. He wanted someone to make sure the snakes stayed in the corner. And time was passing so slowly.

"Bron-wen! What time is it?"

"About a minute later than the last time you asked me, Harvey."

"Yes, but what time is it?"

"2:17 on a Saturday afternoon. In June. You're in your own flat, you took some peyote and you're going to be okay," Bronwen intoned for about the thirtieth time.

Eric turned his head in her direction and managed a feeble "Could I have another glass of water? My mouth is full of dry cotton balls."

All around the room, the crème de la crème of Harvard graduate students lay in various inert clumps, incapacitated by the marvelous cactus cocktail their host had served earlier.

Bronwen, fortunately, had immediately vomited her portion of the foul, moldy smelling brew and so she was both mobile and clear-headed. In point of fact, she was quite enjoying this bizarre turn of events. Queen-for-a-Day of the Egghead Peyote Zombies. Ah, how she could make them suffer if she had a mind to do so!

"Bron-wen, what time is ..."

"Harvey, dammit, it's going to be at least another five hours before this stuff wears off. Just look at your watch if you have to know what time it is." She had never spoken to any of Eric's friends like this before.

"I'm cold, I'm so cold ..." Bronwen was filled with contrition when she saw Harvey's pale, moist face and how his body was rigid with fear. It was so weird, looking down at her host lying on his best Oriental runner on the floor in front of the couch instead of ogling some babe from his usual perch among the itchy cushions.

She poked around in his hall closet and came back with a dusty dark green loden coat, which she draped over his body.

She knelt down to tuck it around his stiff, frail body. It was the closest she'd ever been to Harvey. She caught a surprising whiff of baby talcum powder.

"Thank you. You are the kindest person in the universe. Thank you so much." With that, his eyes rolled back in his head and he tuned out of any remotely shared reality.

Eric, catatonic on the famous alpaca couch, sporadically raised his left arm and tried to make a record of the images and thoughts flooding through his mind. He kept dropping the pencil, but refused to give up his attempt. Days later, Bronwen found the yellow legal pad jammed under a cushion, its top sheet covered with the words:

Baskin-Robbins. Baskin-Robbins. Baskin-Robbins.

Chapter 9

SHE could always tell when her father was drunk because his manners became exaggeratedly polite, then mean and nasty. The waitress would shift in status from "Honey" to "Bitch" between the disappearance of the shrimp cocktails and the appearance of Veal Parmigiana for three—Bronwen, her father and The Girlfriend. The latter usually had recent Toni Home Permanents and long red fingernails. Their names were Sylvia or Charlotte or once, unbelievably enough, Thelma. Thelma had buck teeth and a degree in library science, but her roast beef was never overcooked. The youngest, Marlene, looked like a movie star in her aqua one-piece Cole of California bathing suit and may even briefly have achieved fianceé status. There was a grainy enlargement of a Brownie snapshot of Bronwen at eleven standing next to Marlene on the beach at Fire Island after a hurricane, holding up a two-day-old dead fish that had been thrown up on the beach along with piles of other debris. In the background, the post-storm surf rages. The girl and the much taller young woman (about twenty-two, perhaps) are both pony-tailed and tan, smiling the smiles of 1955. Bronwen was always happy when there was a girlfriend around.

Somehow Marlene disappeared after the next summer, when Bronwen had such bad whooping cough that little chunks of soap-like stuff would come up when she was taken with a fit. She really thought she would die each time the coughing began. Her dad had sublet an unusual split-level furnished apartment on West 12th street for them all, right down the block from an expensive grocery store that carried the most perfect nectarines in the world. The refrigerator full of cold, sweet nectarines and sitting outside in the heat waiting for the day-camp bus to arrive are the only memories Bronwen has of that summer. Sitting in the already hot morning sun, picking at her cuticles and waiting for the stupid bus full of noisy, immature kids. Marlene must not have had such a great summer, either, because she simply faded out of their lives, and the next thing Bronwen knew it was Fall and she and her Dad were shopping at John Wannamaker's for a charcoal gray corduroy skirt and a pink oxford-cloth shirt. That year she even got the impractical white bucks she had been praying for, with pink rubber soles and a little muslin bag of chalky white powder that you were supposed to pat the shoes with when they got smudged. Until she gave up and went with the easy-to-maintain hobo look, soon to be followed by total fashion anarchy in the form of skin-tight black chino skirts, black Danskin tights and filthy white tennis shoes. The beginning of the end, father-daughterwise.

She could be wrong, but she didn't remember traces of any other women after Marlene. The youngest, and the last. And then Bronwen was fifteen, and her father was saying, as they entered his favorite Italian place, "Why don't you call me Roger, instead of Dad, and see if anyone guesses that you're my daughter?" And then he ordered his Four Roses on the rocks and her usual ginger ale. But she didn't call him anything that night. She didn't.

And then she went away to college with her mint-green typewriter portable, rounded and solid as an old Dodge sedan, her Roget's Thesaurus and three new Orlon sweater sets: pink, royal blue and creamy beige. And she stopped writing home, and she stopped calling... Calling him anything. And young men began walking into restaurants with her, and beers were ordered and hamburgers were eaten. And her father was turning fifty and watching Jack Paar until the early hours of the morning, and Marlene, somewhere, was turning thirty.

But best of all is to be nineteen and wearing white Levi's on a summer evening in Cambridge, with a boyfriend who *is* your boyfriend and 24 flavors of Baskin-Robbins ice cream around every corner.

Chapter 10

BRONWEN tried to finish the letter to her father, carrying it back and forth morning and night on the little commuter line that went between Cambridge and Waltham. It became an enormous weight on her conscience. She had avoided seeing him this summer when classes had ended, preferring instead to hop on the first available night flight that would carry her to Boston and Eric's bed. Being entirely faithful to Eric, her first and so far only lover, she had become delirious with sexual longing by June. She was not about to delay their reunion with a stopover in Pasadena at her father's small rented apartment, where he sat nursing his Four Roses and threatening to run off to Tahiti like Gauguin.

"So go if you want to!" she burst out when she was home over Christmas vacation. This only called his bluff and made him more irritable. She, of course, was faking it too because if her father dropped out who would help with college tuition? Couldn't he wait one more year to live his bohemian life, if that's what he wanted? His bitter monologues were torture to her. He knew how anxious she was to stay in school, to get on with her own life. It was cruel, really, the way he hinted that she might have to drop out, that he was about to run out of patience and money. What had he done with that inheritance from his older brother Homer, anyway? Probably lost it all on the stupid stock market. Homer, with his oversized Western belt buckle and his leathery cheeks. He had once given her a narrow, turquoise-studded bracelet with Navajo symbols stamped in the silver. She must have been about eleven. It was her first real jewelry. He had been in New York for a day on some kind of business trip, and they had all gone out for the best Prime Rib in Greenwich Village. Poor Homer. Dropped dead on the floor of Congress, testifying about some water bill on behalf of the Rancher's Association he belonged to. Why couldn't her Dad have turned out like his brother? But then, of course, Homer was dead and her father was still alive.

Thank god she had only one more year and then she wouldn't have to play these humiliating father-daughter mind games. She'd get a grant, teach, do research. In the meantime, she felt like she at least owed him a letter.

She stared out the window, the half-finished page on her lap. It was already outdated. Lines of washing clicked past, women were putting cats out of back doors and kids were already riding tricycles out back on little concrete patios. None of it was relevant to her life, now or in the future. She might never even have children, and she certainly would never live in the dreary suburbs of Boston. The conductor came through, announcing next-stop-Waltham. She sighed and put the stupid letter back in her satchel. Two minutes left to daydream before the day really began. She closed her eyes and imagined Eric slowly letting his weight down on top of her, his compact body vibrating with energy and desire. A double bed and Eric, that was all the Tahiti she needed.

ALL OUT! The dill pickle odor of the creosoted railroad ties, warmed by the morning sun, sharply invaded her awareness. Her nostrils crinkled pleasurably.

She placed one sandaled foot after the other delicately on the gravel piled around the metal tracks, and then briskly increased her stride as she headed up the hill to the lab.

Chapter 11

FROM the clink of test tubes that carried down the long, cluttered hallway, Bronwen knew that Felix was already hard at work. This meant he'd been up all night, since he was never in this early of his own free will. Which in turn meant he'd be grouchy and picky. By 10:30 or so, after planning her day, he'd disappear. She suspected he went out to his battered red VW bug to sleep in the parking lot, judging by his even more rumpled reappearances.

"Aha! She walks in beauty like the night! Or something to that effect. How are you?" Felix scarcely looked up, but kept his stream of patter going while he squinted at the finely calibrated pipettes and expertly moved down the rack of samples, squirting exactly the right amount of radioactive marker chemicals into each test tube. For such a slob, his laboratory technique was exquisite. Bronwen stood quietly to the side of the lab bench until he had finished the row. When he was done, he exhaled and turned to her.

"Whew! It's taken me exactly 13 hours and twenty minutes to get these little suckers to this point. Lemme stick 'em in the incubator and then we can plan your day. Paulette'll think I got locked up in the cold room or something. I couldn't even stop to call her. Disadvantage of working alone." He trundled over to the 37 degree bath and gently lowered the rack of tubes so that the warm water was halfway up their sides. His grimy white shirt was half out of his badly wrinkled khaki pants and one of his klutzy Canadian sandals was coming unbuckled, but his eyes were gleaming with almost unnatural anticipation.

"Can you run these through the scintillation counter in exactly 45 minutes? I'm going to have to go home and take a shower. My sweat is beginning to sweat!" Without waiting for her reply, he rummaged through the mess on top of the small desk that they shared in a corner under the only window in the room. Bronwen's legs were beginning to ache from standing in one place but she knew he would soon be gone and she would be able to sit and collect her thoughts.

"Right. Run the samples, start the new culture and plot my data from last night to see what kind of curve we get. This could be really significant." He looked up and straight into her eyes. She noticed for the first time that they were hazel, flecked with yellow like her father's. His lids were drooping with fatigue. "Then I want you to come up with two alternate theories to explain the results—after which I'll tell you my explanation. Which, of course, is the right one!" He grinned at her and then his face kind of melted, his shoulders sagged and he was suddenly gone. Felix was incredibly light on his feet for such a bulky person.

With Felix gone, things were calmer but the fizz had gone out of the atmosphere. All the odd noises of the laboratory seemed to grow in volume. She heard the gurgle of the pump that kept the water in the incubator bath circulating at 37 degrees, and the hollow whistle of the vacuum system that sucked noxious fumes up into a protective hood (and no doubt spewing them on the innocent citizens of Waltham, Bronwen realized). Above her cluttered gray metal desk, the dusty window panes framed a view of the lush green campus, mostly devoid of under-graduates at this time of year, and an immense sweep of deep, pure blue summer sky. The air conditioner dripped gently just next to her right elbow.

Bronwen began to feel a slight chill, and she hung her satchel on the back of the door. The mysterious Dr. Bergenstrasser's starched white lab coat, usurped for the duration of Bronwen's fellowship, was draped over the back of the desk chair where it had been hastily tossed the night before. She slipped into it, and into her day. If she were lucky, she'd be able to slip away at noon and finish her damn book before Felix reappeared. Everyone in Eric's crowd was reading it and she needed to be able to participate in the discussion if absolutely necessary. But "Homage to Catalonia" was not her idea of lunchtime refreshment, much as she admired George Orwell. She would much rather be reading the nature poems of D.H. Lawrence. In her mind, as she penciled in meticulous dots on Felix's coffee-stained graph paper, she saw David Herbert Lawrence pacing the halls of this unromantic cement-block building, pounding on the EXIT doors and finally escaping to throw himself down on the large patch of dandelions that she could see out of the corner of her eye.

A harsh "BRRING!" from the timer sent her pulse skittering and she rushed over with a green styrofoam bucket packed almost to the top with finely crushed ice. She lifted the rack of tubes up with her left hand and with her other plunged the tubes one by one into the ice bucket on the countertop, abruptly halting the biochemical reaction that Felix had set in motion. She started towards the side room where the radioactivity in the samples was to be measured, telling them how much new enzyme the virus had produced after infecting its host. Then she heard the familiar, passionately whistled version of Beethoven's Violin Concerto in D wafting down the hall. RATS! Felix was back already.

"Couldn't sleep! Too curious about the results!" He was freshly shaven, his crisp light blue shirt was tucked in, and he smelled faintly of bacon. The hair on his forearms was so clean it was actually fuzzy, like a newborn baby's head after its first shampoo. "Paulette made me coffee and eggs and I got a second wind. I can take over now."

She stepped back and watched as he decanted the contents of the tubes into the vials that would be sealed and then sent down a conveyor belt to be scanned inside the chamber of the radiation monitor. He desperately needed a haircut. Unruly wet curls were bunched over his ears and soaking his shirt collar. At least he was clean for a change.

Without turning around or missing a beat in the steady rhythm of filling the vials, Felix startled her by asking, "You free for lunch? We could save time and bring the data with us. Maybe even sit out on the grass."

Saved. Anything but Orwell. He must have read her mind.

"Sure. That would be okay. Let me complete the graph while you finish that up."

She hurried back to the desk, her spirits lighter. Strange how easy it was to be around Felix now, after the tension of the first few weeks. It wasn't like being with Eric and Harvey and the rest. With Felix, she had nothing to gain or lose. After this summer, she'd probably never see him again. Of course, she needed his letter of recommendation for graduate school, but she felt that was already in the bag and it was all downhill cruising from here on. Provided she didn't screw up in any major way. That possibility seemed unlikely. Her future loomed ahead, as cheerful as the bright green grass and yellow dandelions of this glorious day.

It was only later in the afternoon that she realized Felix had never asked her to present and justify her two theories. That gave her an extra day to prepare, and she packed several reprints into her satchel so she could do some extra reading before she went to bed.

She arrived back at the apartment a little after six-thirty, perspiring and smudged with grime from the train. It had been running late and she had galloped home from the station, dimly aware that she was supposed to be ready to leave again by seven but not recalling why.

"Finally! Didn't I tell you last night my parents had invited us to dinner at the place where they're staying? We're supposed to be there no later than 7." Eric was in a state.

"Of course I remember. It's not my fault the train was late. I will be *ready*." In fact, she had totally forgotten that Eric's parents had arrived for their yearly visit to Boston. As she spoke, she was ripping off her clothes and heading for the shower. Please, let them not bring up the subject of Orwell and I'll be fine.

Little did she know that was to be her last coherent thought for the evening.

Chapter 12

"SO, what are you kids drinking tonight? Vodka? Gin and tonic? White wine? Cream sherry?"

The dinner party was being put on at the Aronsons, in Boston. They and Eric's parents went way back.

Harvey, a favorite of theirs among Eric's friends, was there too. He never missed a chance at a good free meal. Tonight Bronwen was very glad to see his boyish, pudgy face when she walked in the door. They had formed a subtle bond of attachment since the day of the peyote fiasco, although they had an unspoken pact never to make reference to the incident.

Eric's father, Sam, had been nominated to do the bartending honors. He waited for Bronwen to make her choice.

She hesitated, contemplating the proper drink for a girlfriend to request. She was not familiar with anything stronger than Harvey's famous jug reds. Sam continued gazing patiently at her.

He had a full head of crinkly gray hair and smooth pink cheeks. Her own rapidly balding father would give his right foot for hair like that. (You could still do the breaststroke with one foot, couldn't you?)

They were all staring at her now.

"Uh.. vodka would be fine."

"Okay-dokey. Whoops! I take that back, we seem to be out of tonic, young lady. Or would you like that on the rocks?" He turned around, eyebrows wiggling high on his forehead.

"Dad!"

"Sure. That would be fine." Bronwen pressed her hands hard against her empty stomach, which was beginning to gurgle.

"Really! If you say so ..."

"DAD ..." Eric was glaring at his father now.

"No, really, that will be fine. Yes, with a twist of lime, great. I'm really thirsty." She took the proffered glass and emptied it in three swallows. In moments her throat began to glow. Then her rib cage expanded and every seam of her linen shift pressed itself into her flesh. She was a pillar of fire.

Sam continued to gaze at her, but she could think of nothing to say. Sam glanced over at Eric as if asking for approval—or forgiveness.

"Well, that's quite a woman you have there. Here's your sherry, Eric. The usual, Harvey?"

"Children! Dinner's ready! It's my first Coq au Vin, in honor of Eric's friend!"

They all trooped into the dining room, Bronwen following last. She placed one foot carefully in front of the other and thanked the gods she had worn flat sandals instead of her pumps with the little stiletto heels.

Somehow she dished herself some noodles and fragrant chicken stew, again glad she was wearing black in case she dribbled. Not looking to the right or left, she concentrated on the task at hand: getting the fork to and from her mouth without tipping the contents into her lap. Her eyeballs felt like lead marbles, and her tongue seemed to have enlarged fivefold.

"Kids! What do they know anymore! They know from nothing about politics! And history! Forget about history! They don't even know the first thing about Sacco and Vanzetti!" There was a burst of scornful laughter from Sam's captive audience, including Bronwen. Sam was in his element. He turned to her, interrupting her giggles. Her head was drooping somewhat in an attempt to make herself invisible, but she had laughed as loud as the rest.

"So, tell me, amazing young lady, what do *YOU* know about Sacco and Vanzetti?"

There was complete silence. Harvey dropped his fork and as he leaned over to get it, whispered into her ear:

"Italian Anarchists. Framed by mob. Scapegoats. Landmark case."

She tried to formulate a sentence about oppressed Italian goat farmers, but that didn't seem right. It was no use. She was doomed. The vodka had paralyzed every nerve in her body.

With superhuman effort she managed to utter human speech.

"I'm afraid I am unable to speak at the present moment. Thank you. I'm very sorry."

Sam was no sadist. He simply spread his hands, raised his eyes to the heavens in the classic "What did I tell you?" and resumed eating. The two older women bustled around collecting empty plates and bringing out cheesecake and coffee cups.

The worst part was, nobody looked in her direction for the remainder of the meal. Sam shook hands warmly as they left, but kept his eyes averted.

* * * *

If Eric had at least criticized her, yelled at her, been sarcastic, she could have borne it. But the silence in the car on the way home was unbearable. First they dropped off Harvey, who like Einstein didn't drive, and continued on to their apartment. When Eric had parked and was on his way up the stairs, she finally had a moment of clarity. She stood unmoving on the sidewalk.

"I'll be back in a little while. I need some air."

"Fine with me," Eric muttered, without bothering to turn around. "I'll leave the door unlocked."

Bronwen wandered aimlessly for a few blocks, mentally slicing her brains to ribbons with the Swiss Army knife that Felix kept in his top desk drawer. She imagined a small fire beginning at her feet that ignited into a roaring blaze with her at the center, consuming her and leaving a neat pile of pale gray ashes the color of Sam's hair. She pictured Sam and Felix staring down at her remains, shaking their heads. Eric was nowhere to be seen.

Self-disgust pounded through her veins, and collected behind her throbbing temples. Not only was she Ignorant, capital I, she was also a Phoney. If only she hadn't laughed along with the others. She could have sweetly asked Sam for a history lesson instead of being exposed as a mindless fool and hypocrite.

She passed a taxi, motor idling near the Porter Square train station, waiting for the final trickle of potential fares. Impulsively, she pulled open the door and slid in. The leather seat was pleasantly cool against her bare legs. She had fifty dollars in her purse, having cashed her Friday paycheck at noon that day.

"Waltham, please. I have to check on an experiment."

The cabbie checked her out in his rearview mirror. He raised one eyebrow and started his meter. He radiated disapproval. She knew what he was thinking: Not enough make-up for a hooker but you never know what these professors go for ...

She didn't care. It was getting really boring, worrying what people thought about her all the time. One thing about vodka, as the most debilitating effects began to wear off she was starting to feel pretty damn good.

The landscape was different by night and by cab. She felt mysterious and important. She would show Eric and the rest of them that she had a mind, that she wasn't just a long-haired bimbo with good legs. Well of course Eric didn't consider her a bimbo, good grief, but why did she always feel so stupid when he was around? Did he ever do anything more than quote some essay in *The New Republic*, or repeat a line from an old Groucho Marx movie? Was that intelligence?

There were no women and children, not even any barking dogs out tonight. Only a few other cars, and the ribbon of black asphalt. The smaller side road leading to the University was lined on both sides with graceful Lombardy poplars, their leaves glistening in the headlights of the taxi. The only sounds were the whoosh of the cab's tires and the dark masses of leaves rustling in the night air.

Bronwen realized that she had never traveled by car to the lab, and it didn't feel like she was going to the same old familiar place. It was more like a rendezvous with a lover.

Chapter 13

AS SHE paid the driver and stepped out into the deserted parking lot, Bronwen joyfully remembered the old canvas cot that Felix kept stacked behind his desk. She could sleep here tonight. When Felix arrived in the morning, she'd already have an experiment underway. Wouldn't he be surprised!

Paulette heard the soft click of the front door lock closing. Her body was rigid as she waited for Felix to appear in the doorway of their bedroom. She heard the refrigerator door open and close, and then the sound of vigorous toothbrushing. When the partially open bedroom door began to slowly move inwards, she sat up. At the first sight of his face, she let him have it.

"I can't take this anymore! I never know where you are or when you'll be home! How can you even think about having this baby! You don't even know if you'll have a job next year!"

"Paulette, I ..."

"No! There's nothing you can say. What if I don't get my grant? Who's going to pay the rent? Do you know how expensive childcare is? Even if I get my grant how am I going to be able to work? And my blood pressure is up. The doctor said at my age I should be taking it easy and staying off my feet. Ha! He's not married to you!"

"Paulette, you're ..."

"No! Don't try to humor me. Everything's fucked up! Everything!" Her tears were unstoppable. She shrieked and threw herself back on the bed, fists pounding the mattress at her sides and sobbing one huge sob after another.

Felix backed out of the doorway, and down the hall, never taking his eyes off the bedroom door. He fumbled for his keys in the little Chinese dish on the hall table, turned the doorknob with his hand twisted behind his back, and exited. He stood in the hallway of the building for a moment, then gently closed the apartment door. For several moments Felix stood there, keys in hand, listening to the sound of his own breathing. Then he turned and walked out into the night.

On the way to the lab, he formed a plan. He would collect his papers, leave a note for Bronwen, and fly to Canada tomorrow night. He'd stay with his old professor there, as long as he needed to in order to finish those experiments and ensure his tenure. For tonight, he could sleep on the old canvas cot he kept for napping during all-night experiments. In the morning, he'd leave a note for Paulette. It was better if he didn't see her in person until he had some progress to report. It all seemed logical and reasonable. She was right, their situation was precarious. To be fair, the baby hadn't been his idea. She couldn't really blame him for adding that parameter to the equation of their lives.

He parked his VW in the usual slot, a short walk to the basement vending machines, and stopped for the usual two packages of peanut-butter filled cheese crackers. These and a Coke from the upstairs frig would do for breakfast. Whistling, he took the stairs two at a time. Strangely, he wasn't even tired. He felt excited about taking up the gauntlet Paulette had thrown down, and getting his life in order. Sometimes you just needed a good kick in the pants.

Without turning on the lights, he strode quickly into the lab and headed directly for his desk. It was important to try to get some sleep. He would collapse on the cot and collect his things in the morning. At that instant he felt a blinding pain in his shins and for the second time in a single evening, a female was shrieking at him, this time only inches from his left eardrum.

Chapter 14

OMIGOD. The janitor was trying to rape her! Reflexively, Bronwen did the only thing that came to her sleep-sodden mind: she opened her mouth wide and bit down hard on the big hairy arm from Hell that had landed on her face. "Help! Help! Fire!" she yelled somewhat inanely, as taught.

"Ow! Stop it! Bronwen, it's o.k., it's Felix! Stop, goddammit. Ow!" Her attacker fell back when she released her teeth, but didn't flee. Indeed, it was Felix.

Seeing her still terrorized face, he stopped swearing and started apologizing from where he sat, flopped on the floor beside the cot.

"I'm sorry I scared you, but Jesus H. Christ, I'm going to need a tetanus shot now. And my leg hurts like a motherf ..." He looked warily at the still speechless Bronwen. Although sitting, he somehow managed to rock back and forth,

Felixlike even in distress. Especially in distress. He looked glumly at the reddening circle of indentations on his forearm, then up at her.

She just kept staring at him in disbelief.

"I SAID I'm sorry if I scared you. But anyway, what were you doing in my bed ...Miss ...Goldilocks, I presume?"

At that he exploded in a whoop of off-balance laughter. He looked at his arm and howled. Tears streamed down his cheeks, and finally his manic mood became contagious.

"Argument with Eric ..." explained Bronwen, and doubled over.

"Yeah ... fight with Paulette," managed Felix, and he rolled over flat onto his back. "Hoo. Hoo ha. Oh boy."

By now, the rectangles of glass above Felix's desk were pale violet. A thin blue light seeped into the room. The clock over the incubator showed it to be 5:37 in the morning.

"What say we hit world-famous Dunkin' Donuts on Main and then come back and get organized? Felix's eyes were bloodshot but his voice was as buoyant as ever.

"Only if you let me buy this round. I'm loaded- payday, you know. And I definitely have to wash first." Bronwen sat up and swung her legs over the edge of the cot. Her linen dress was a horror. Luckily, this was not the kind of detail that Felix would notice or care two figs about.

"You're on. I want a large coffee, too, I'm giving you fair warning. And let's bring the log book. We need to plan your week since I'm going to be away. I did tell you I was flying to Toronto, didn't I?" He knew he hadn't, but didn't want her to think he was running away in haste.

He paced in the corner, waiting. It didn't occur to him that he should also freshen up, beyond running his hands once through his tangled curls. His arm still throbbed, but he decided to forego the shots—too embarrassing. The toothmarks were so obviously human.

Felix noticed that the sky outside was now streaked with palest yellow and rose. Birds were twittering their little beaks off. While Bronwen continued to do female things in the bathroom, he folded the trusty old cot and stacked it behind his desk. He grabbed the gray looseleaf binder and lumbered down the hall to the stairwell. When Bronwen emerged and walked quickly toward the corner where Felix was now standing, he thought for a second it was three summers ago, and it was Paulette floating, floating just after the first time of making love under his desk.

He controlled the powerful impulse to take Bronwen's hand. This was not Paulette. Not wife, not girlfriend. In a mock gallant gesture, he motioned to her to proceed down the stairs ahead of him. He didn't want to make small talk.

His bones felt suddenly tired, very tired and brittle, and his brain seemed very, very small. Only his heart felt huge.

Chapter 15

"ARE you having an affair with Felix?" She had never seen Eric angry like this: out-front, loud, ANGRY.

"Are you *crazy?*" Bronwen meant her question quite literally, not rhetorically. Eric must have snapped. Some male ego-turf-hormone paranoia thing had twisted his mind.

"Well, I demand a minimal explanation of where you've been. I deserve that much, at least."

It was lunchtime, and Eric had crossed paths with Bronwen just as Felix was driving away after dropping her off. Eric was munching on a mammoth Reuben sandwich that was partially protruding from its waxed paper cocoon. The sides overflowed with pastrami, and there was a tiny piece of sauerkraut on his nose. They walked inside together, and Eric pulled the other half of the Reuben out of the soggy brown paper bag and put it on a cutting board that was lying on the kitchen table. Bronwen's eyes kept returning to that glorious vision as Eric droned on.

"I was worried about you, if you didn't know. If you weren't home by noon I was going to call the police, for Chrissake." The fragment of sauerkraut was sliding towards his nostril.

Bronwen cleared her throat. It was now or never.

"Could I have the other half of your sandwich?"

Eric looked shocked, then sly. "Sure ...if you fuck me first." His eyes had that slightly cross-eyed look he got when he was horny.

She nodded, and he reached for her but she was already on her way into the bedroom. Somehow one of them pulled her dress off without unzipping it, and they were entangled together. The eloquent speech she had been going to make about individual freedom and dignity had flown from her mind.

If only she could possess two bodies. One would be at the service of her intellect—a low-maintenance, E-Z Care Bronwen who slept, ate and worked tirelessly. A good old reliable Bronwen.

The other Bronwen would spend all her days in bed, stroking and rolling and pushing and licking. Yes. Oh yes.

"Shit!" Eric blurted. "Is it 12:30 already? I have a one o'clock

Barbara Riddle

tutorial. See you tonight, pruneface. Enjoy the sandwich!"

He was gone in a rumble of motorcycle exhaust. The sheets smelled of sauerkraut and sperm.

A sudden clank of the letterflap signaled the mailman's arrival and departure. She put on Eric's old maroon terrycloth bathrobe with the Harvard crest on the breast pocket and wandered out to the living room. Just inside the front door was a long, pale blue envelope. Must be from California. Her father always used Air Mail stationery. She walked over and picked it up. It was thicker than usual, and on the front he had carefully printed DO NOT BEND in big block letters. Curious now, she brought it into the kitchen to read while she polished off the now cold and unpleasantly greasy sandwich.

Chapter 16

WHEN she opened the envelope, carefully slitting it along the top edge with a nail file that was lying on the kitchen table, an unsmiling black and white passport-size snapshot of her father fell onto the table, taped to a piece of torn shirt cardboard. The letter itself, on paper that matched the envelope, was brief, almost too short for the large old-fashioned loops and swirls that were the last remaining vestige of his Oklahoma childhood:

Dear Bronwen:

I write to wish you all the best. You surely deserve a good life. Enclosed please find a recent picture. Take care of yourself.

Sincerely, Daddy

Weird. And no cheque. She had expected some sort of "Enjoy your summer" note and some bucks to spend on a new bathing suit or sandals. Oh well, she didn't really need the money anyway. Apparently even the pittance she was getting as a summer intern was more than her father was earning these days.

Bronwen stood up, crumpling the greasy paper wrapper from Eric's sandwich and tossing it in the overflowing garbage pail. She and Eric were having a contest to see who could last the longest in tolerating a dirty kitchen. Correction. A filthy kitchen. The loser had to spring for a five-course banquet at the Taj Mahal, off Porter Square. She had high hopes for a victory within the week. It was that or call an exterminator.

First a shower, then maybe a walk down to Harvard Square to try and find a copy of an obscure novel called *Notebooks of Malte Laurids Brigge* to further her self-imposed Rilke project. She deserved a day off and she was too tired and stiff to even consider going into the lab. But when Felix left for Canada, she fantasized as she dropped her robe on the floor of the bathroom and stepped behind the moldy shower curtain, she was going to try something different.

The idea for the new series of experiments had been simmering ever since she had talked to Professor Baldessori after his stimulating (in every sense of the word) seminar last week.

Was it only six days ago that she had been sitting in that cool, braincell-crammed room? It truly seemed like weeks. Which was odd, because she was far from bored. Time wasn't dragging—experience was accumulating. Maybe it had something to do with riding the train twice a day. She had never really believed that stuff about being younger on arrival if you traveled at the speed of light...come on, who was Albert kidding? Give her good old reliable biochem anyday, where all you had to do was repeat, repeat, repeat. Yes, all you physicists, eat your hearts out, repent and repeat, join the crowd and loosen up. Do a real touchy-feely experiment for a change.

She stepped out from behind the curtain and grabbed the nearest—and only—towel. It was still damp from Eric's morning shower. Ugh. As she wrapped it around her and padded into the bedroom to dress, Bronwen realized she had just proven to herself that time expands when you're having fun. Like the elastic on an old pair of underpants. You could do more stuff, remember more if you liked what you were doing. Be on the Pill, gain weight and still fit in the same old undies. Not that she felt like getting dressed yet.

She dropped the towel on the floor and picked up her brush from the morass on top of the dresser. For the 800th time she reflected on how much she liked sleeping with Eric. It wasn't as if she had, or wanted, any grounds for comparison. She sat on the unmade bed, brushing her hair and enjoying the gusts of tepid air that blew in from the open window on her clean, still-damp body.

An affair with Felix? Hardly. He was practically middle-aged, fat, and married.

She wandered over, minus towel, to the stereo in the dimly lit living room. They kept the curtains drawn to block the worst of the afternoon sun from overheating their small flat. Still on the turntable was a Heifetz recording of two Bach Partitas for Unaccompanied Violin that Eric was studying. She turned on the power and, ever so carefully balancing the tone arm on the pad of her forefinger, she lowered the needle to the narrow blank groove at the outer rim of the spinning vinyl. In a few seconds, the music erupted in full, agonizing glory. It was the same piece that he played the night he first invited her to his room, almost three years ago. What a calculating Lothario he had been. She smiled. "Mind if I practice before we go out?" Ha! They had never made it to the movie.

That was the first time Bronwen had ever been in the same room with a real violin, and certainly the first time in a room containing both a violin and an exposed prick. An unbeatable combination, apparently.

They hadn't made love that night, though. He had been too stunned when, as he started to remove her underpants, he casually said, "So, you're not a virgin, right?" and she replied that she was.

"What!" He moved away from her and began trying to stuff himself back into his Levi's. His face was a purplish crimson. "But I thought you said you were from Greenwich Village!"

People always asked her why she stayed faithful to him for so long. How could she explain that when she went to his bed, she was sleeping with Bach, with Brecht, with Science. Eric was so sure of his world and of himself. Being with him was like walking at night in a park with the scrappiest bulldog in town. It actually made her lightheaded sometimes, seeing how people were afraid of his mind. And she never tired of the moment when he lost control inside her, became for a few seconds warm and affectionate and tender. In her power for a change. None of his friends ever saw him that way. It was her secret. So far, it was enough.

Bronwen continued to stand dreamily in the dark living room of their Cambridge flat while Heifetz showered her with brilliance, his own and Bach's. Her heart pounded with the same excitement always evoked by the twists and turns that seemed to emanate from a roomful of instruments, but in fact streamed forth from a single violin.

There was no one to bear witness, but there were actual Bach-induced goosebumps on her bare ass.

Meanwhile, on the floor of the steamed-up bathroom, the ink on her father's letter, poking out from the pocket of the terrycloth bathrobe, ran and smeared in a shallow puddle on the tile floor, trailing thin swirls of blue in the warm water that smelled faintly of Breck shampoo.

Chapter 17

"WHO'S THERE?" A startled Dr. Bergenstrasser whirled around, clutching a folded lab coat whose whiteness almost matched her face.

"I'm sorry .... I didn't mean to frighten you." Bronwen herself felt little shocks of alarm tingling all over her body.

"Well, you are obviously scaring the shit from out of me. Have they got *you* spying on me, also?"

Although Bronwen had never seen Dr. Bergenstrasser in person before and had no earthly idea what she could be referring to, she had known immediately who this statuesque woman was. What to say, what to do? For the present, Bronwen simply tried to keep her eyes off the neatly folded-under and safety-pinned empty sleeve where Inge's left arm wasn't. She recalled now some story about Dr. Bergenstrasser fleeing Germany as a young woman, serving with honor in the Israeli army and then emigrating to the United States.

And oh yes, she remembered now some gossip about a current problem related to Inge's inability to repeat the Chairman's most recent series of experiments. Inge noticed Bronwen's bewildered expression and gave her a twisted smile.

"Yes, I am again a casualty. Just because I tell it like I see it. I never said he lied, I just said that Inge Bergenstrasser could not get those results. No, not ever, I think. And his solution? I am to go! Only Felix believes me and he cannot afford to get mixed up in this. Better he should disappear for awhile. Especially with the baby coming. He needs the job more than I. For me, my mother and I have enough. It was never for money that I did this work. No, never for the money. Not Felix, either. But what will become of either of us?"

All the while she talked, Dr. Bergenstrasser was packing books into the small cardboard boxes that littered her lab bench. Into boxes extolling the virtues of Smirnoff vodka went heavy tomes on embryology, biochemistry, molecular biology and biophysics. Bronwen just continued to stand there awkwardly. Felix had never mentioned Paulette's pregnancy. And what if he was just running away to Canada to wait until the controversy about Inge blew over? For all his faults, she had never thought he would be capable of hypocrisy. Or outright cowardice. And what if he didn't come back?

She had never really given two seconds' thought to the vague rumors about Dr. Bergenstrasser's predicament until today. Watching her pack, the empty sleeve swinging vigorously as she moved briskly along the lab bench, taking down postcards of Italian frescoes and squeezing dusty textbooks into the gaudy boxes, Bronwen felt certain that this woman was telling the truth and that a grave injustice was being done. She vowed she would convince Felix to take a stand when he came back from his trip.

Feeling like a cross between Madame Curie and Doris Day, Bronwen excused herself and hurried over to her corner of the room. On the desk, sticking out from her gray lab notebook, was a note in scarlet Magic Marker from, of course, Felix:

Hi, Bronzie! We from North of the Border salute you and entreat you to carry on! Surprise and delight me—if you dare.

I'll be back when I'm back (said the Cheshire cat).

Your globetrotting mentor, F.

Sheesh. She was on her own. Sooner than she had expected. Bronwen opened the book to a clean page and logged in: July

4, 1963.

She could only hope—praying was not in her lexicon—that the Italian's theory was more than a plate of cold spaghetti. It was worth two days of her time to find out, anyway. The door banged shut; Dr. Bergenstrasser and the cart loaded with boxes were gone.

Bronwen realized that she hadn't even offered to help, not wanting to imply any insufficiency on the Professor's part. Maybe Inge thought she was not discreet, just an asshole. Why was it sometimes impossible to figure out how to behave with simple decency?

It wasn't too difficult to see why people like Felix preferred to have the rules laid out neatly for them. Did most scientists feel a silent bond, a shared passionate thirst for Logic and Truth and Meaning? Because secretly they didn't have a clue. And the main difference between them and the average person was that the scientists at least *KNEW* they didn't really have a clue. But what kind of person was she? Bronwen tried to imagine Felix, Inge and Eric having dinner together, thirsting away, but the images refused to coalesce. The three didn't seem to share the same planet, much less the same profession.

Better just to get the experiment going and leave the moralizing for the train ride home.

Chapter 18

CLICKETY-click, clickety-clack. It was like a Bogart flick, with an unsolved mystery, a suspect and a broad. Bronwen stared out the window at the usual drab assortment of backyard life, but her eyes looked inward and her pulse was racing.

She was the dame, the suspect was her virus, and the mystery was how the virus could take over the bacterial host and cause thousands of copies of itself to be made, using the host's machinery. Kind of like a gorgeous model walking into a sweatshop in the garment district with a loaded gun and forcing all the seamstresses to knock off copies of the Chanel suit she's wearing, until the suits fill the room to the brim, suffocating the workers and bursting the walls of the room; in this case, the suits are also filled with identical, beautiful models, who run down the halls of the factory and into other rooms, demanding at gunpoint that more copies of the suits get made ...etc. But what was the gun, in this case?

The conductor swung by, punched the ticket she had stuck into the rim of the seat in front of her, and continued. He was used to glassy-eyed students riding home late on the train, but not usually on the Fourth of July.

Bronwen's head ached. It was the Italian's theory that the virus—the couture model—came in with instructions for making an item that only it could use, say some special accessory, like trademark Chanel buttons for the suit jacket. The seamstresses then had no choice but to make the garments that used those buttons; the old outfits they had been working on just couldn't be made with those buttons. Everything else they needed—cloth, patterns, lining material—was right there. So, Chanel suits it was. In this case, the suit "button" was a special version of one of the four basic components of the virus DNA. And the discovery she'd made was that the virus stimulated the host to make an enzyme that produced lots of these special bases. As if an ordinary button was being transformed into the Chanel button by stamping it with little back to back "C'"s. It was so diabolical! Taking over and destroying your host, but first getting it to make the item you need to wreak your destruction! And the information for creating your new "buttons" comes in with your own DNA—you have the smarts, you just don't have the seamstresses or the buttons. You--you gorgeous little virus, you—you're just a swirl of DNA wrapped in a little old protein coat for protection.

Today was the first time anyone—she, Bronwen!—had shown how this particular virus was able to take over its host and turn it into a me-first virus factory. Other scientists had observed similar events in other host-virus systems, so the discovery wasn't earth-shattering, but it would help to prove a general rule. Bring them closer to understanding how DNA expresses itself in the exquisite choreography of a dividing embryo, or goes haywire in lethal, uncontrollable cancers. Mr. Cohen would burst a button on his lab coat if he only knew. The whole damn eighth grade would stand up and cheer!

Bronwen felt bodiless and weightless. She barely heard the conductor call out her stop, and she didn't even remember turning up her street or how she got into the apartment. It was pitch dark. When she finally turned on the hall light, she realized that she'd forgotten all about the Harvard-M.I.T. Annual Softball Jamboree. Thank God. That also meant Eric wouldn't be back until much later. It was strange, not having anyone to tell about her discovery. She reminded herself that anyone could have carried out the experiment once it was suggested. But she had bothered to do it, and she had done it carefully, and she knew, she could feel it in all her bones, that her finding was correct. She hugged the feeling to her. Part of her wanted to wallow in this sensation of private knowledge for as long as possible; another part wanted to shout it from the rooftops.

It was impossible to sleep. These feelings were utterly new to her. Was she a scientist now? Was there a line that you crossed? She had set her trap, and snared her prey. She and Nature were becoming bosom buddies. Although actually, it felt more like female mud wrestling. This was hard, and scary. This wasn't like getting the right answer on a test. This was... falling through a hole in the surface of things. Lifting the veil. Wow. Just as well Eric wasn't here. He would probably sneer at her. Felix was the one she wanted to talk to. And he was in Canada somewhere, wuffling around in someone else's lab. A pang of incompleteness—of Felixlessness—flickered through her before she fell into a deep and profoundly sweet sleep.

Chapter 19

"PAUL-EE? Are you awake? Rejoice! It is I, your one and only love slave!" Felix dropped his canvas carry-all in the entryway, disgorging dirty socks and a copy of Cell Biology. He stepped down hard and almost flipped over onto his back, skidding on the pile of loose envelopes—bills, science journals and junk mail—that lay strewn just inside the door. His plan had been to surprise Paulette by appearing without calling first, but the house smelled stale and felt very empty. This was not his idea of a good time. It was after midnight, time for all pregnant wives to be home in bed. Especially *his* pregnant wife. Where was she?

He tiptoed down the hall, but things didn't get any better. In their bedroom, the uninhabited bed was a vast wasteland; the naif Adam and Eve on the handpainted Indian bedspread mocked him in their sweet sensuality. Precisely over the spot where the artist had drawn the Forbidden Apple was a note from Paulette:

Gone fishing. Doctor says bed rest essential. Maine cooler than Boston; parents happy to take me in. Please water the damn plants (especially begonia).
You know my number.

I'm not mad, just confused. Whatever you do, don't come up. Hope you had good luck in Canada.
P.S. Inge's in deep shit. Also, rumor has it that Bronwen might be onto something interesting.

P.P.S. We really need to talk when I get back.

He let the note drift out of his hands onto the floor. There was nothing he could do about any of it at this hour. Exhaustion weighed on him, sucked the last breath out of his body, and he simply sat down, leaned back and passed out.

Felix slept badly and woke at dawn, soaked in sweat and desperately needing to take a leak. What did Paulette mean by saying Bronwen was up to something? Did she find evidence that Inge, and not the Chairman, had been the one faking data? After all the Memos he had written in her support?

He staggered to the bathroom, then stumbled down the hallway to find his bag and some aspirin. In the dark, he found himself slipping and sliding and began to hope this was only a nightmare. As he felt himself go down, he recalled the pile of loose magazines and bills at the entrance. Done in by *The Nation*, he thought ruefully, as his ankle twisted under him with an ugly popping sound.

The next thing he was conscious of was the ringing of the hall phone. Daylight poured in through the panes of the front door. His leg was one gargantuan cylinder of throbbing agony. The phone kept ringing, and he managed to drag himself over to it and grab the receiver.

"Felix? I'm sorry to bother you at home but I remembered you said you'd be back today and I wondered if we could ride to the lab together. There're some things I want to tell you. Did I wake you up?"

Felix, wheezing with relief, explained his predicament to the horrified Bronwen. She insisted on taking a taxi right over and going with him to the Cambridge Emergency Room.

He hung up, dragged himself over to the front door and unlocked it, checked to make sure his fly was zipped up and then lay panting on his back. He debated the merits of calling Paulette but decided not to. Then, between spasms of severe pain emanating from that huge geographical area that had formerly been a mere ankle, he recognized another intense sensation: anger.

Afterwards, tearing into a warm Apple Fritter at Dunkin' Donuts, Felix listened while Bronwen told him about the excitement of corroborating Baldessori's hunch. Already high on painkillers, he was practically levitating at the implications. "If it's true, then we'll get a paper out of this! I can present the results at the October Federation Meetings!"

"If it's true?" Bronwen's joyful expression was rapidly fading.

"My little chickadee, even bright young things like yourself should know that we have to confirm results as many ways as we can. This time, instead of tracking the disappearance of one thing, we'll look for the appearance of the new stuff. I'll show you how, if you'll do the footwork for me. I'm ready when you are."

"Right now? Aren't you supposed to be off your feet?"

"I will be, don't worry. You're going to do all the work. Let's go. And bring two more Maple Bars, will you? I'll pay you later. You do trust me, don't you?"

This was all a bit more than she had expected. It was already midafternoon and she knew it was going to be a long night. And what if her results didn't hold up under his scrutiny? They emerged and scanned Harvard Square for yet another cab. Bronwen was embarrassed to note that Felix had a glop of apple filling on the front of his shirt. It wasn't all that surprising that Paulette had gone off to Maine for a little tranquillity. She wondered if he had anyone else to talk to.

As they clambered into the taxi and Felix gave directions, Bronwen thought for a second that it was the same damn driver who had leered at her the night she had drunkenly fled Cambridge after the fight with Eric. But no.

"Hey," she turned towards Felix on a sudden whim. "You know a lot of weird stuff. Tell me about Sacco and Vanzetti."

Felix wiped his sticky hands on his wrinkled chinos. This girl was totally unpredictable. It wasn't as if she were stupid, but she made him feel so damn smart.

"Glad you asked." And for the next forty-five minutes Felix was in heaven, ankle and flyaway wife forgotten.

Hours later, she called Eric to tell him she'd be working late because Felix, in spite of his twisted ankle, was helping her confirm her results. It looked like her conclusions were going to bear up under scrutiny!

Eric scathingly replied that if she stayed in the lab all evening she would miss the champagne celebration in the Biology department to honor his appointment as a Harvard Junior Fellow. And he hung up on her.

Chapter 20

BEING at a concert with Felix was, no doubt about it, humiliating in the extreme. He had insisted she accompany him so that Paulette's ticket wouldn't go to waste (she was still visiting her parents in Maine, he said) and besides, she deserved a night off.

They'd been working night and day, practically, confirming Bronwen's discovery and Felix was seen clomping along the halls of the biochem building at odd hours, beaming with mentorly pride and boasting at great lengths about his Socratic teaching skills to anyone within hearing range who was verifiably awake. It was not necessary to show interest, merely to be breathing and/or moving. He had become so notorious that Harold, the night janitor, literally dropped his broom and ran when he spied Felix at the end of the corridor. This Bronwen saw with her own eyes as she was coming out of the Ladies' Room at 11:30 the previous evening.

Although flattered by his obvious excitement and pride, she was beginning to feel as though credit was siphoning off in his direction, like cold air being drawn up towards the warmer layer of gas at the top of a chamber. A polite way of saying that Felix was in danger of becoming an annoying windbag. Then, just as she was about to speak her mind to him, he presented her with a first edition of George Orwell's *Animal Farm*, wrapped in the Sunday funnies. Tucked under the string tying it together was the concert ticket and a note: "Some summer interns are more equal than others. You are the more equalest. Congratulations. We've been lucky to have you."

She couldn't very well have said no, and anyway it was Eric's softball night. So here they were, Felix rocking back and forth in his seat, sweating like (as they say) a pig, and Bronwen trying to ignore the glares of the silver-haired Harvard faculty wives who surrounded them. Oblivious, Felix loudly kept time by tapping his left foot on the stone floor of the old chapel that doubled as a recital hall. One ankle was still an ugly yellowish-blue. (He was wearing his best black dress shoes but he had forgotten to wear socks.)

It was one of the late Beethoven quartets, intense and tortured, not like the delicate Brahms that Eric and his friends attempted weekly in their apartment. The atmosphere was humid and close, in spite of the windows thrown open to catch any hint of a breeze on this warm Cambridge evening. The honking of horns and an occasional fire engine punctuated the throbbing waves of music, and the whole effect was stupefying. Bronwen's mind kept disengaging and wandering. Several questions recurred:

1) Why did men keep trying to get her to read Orwell? (At least *Animal Farm* was easier going than that damn memoir Eric had urged on her, which she had grimly renamed *Homage to Catatonia.*)

2) Would she get home in time to be able to make love to Eric before he went to sleep? It had been three nights without and the summer was shrinking away all too fast.

3) When would be the right time to ask Felix for advice about graduate school, without seeming too much of a suck-up?

She was brought back from her reverie by the wild applause, not least due to the efforts of her concertmate, and his shouts of "Encore! Encore!" As he stood up, she pressed herself tightly to the back of the oak pew, whose ancient varnish was somewhat sticky from the heat of her bare arms and legs.

Maybe no one would guess that they were together. She sneaked a peek at him. His cheeks were flaming pink, glowing, and he looked like a near-sighted cherub in a wrinkled white shirt. God's accountant or something. She hoped Paulette loved him. He would probably be a magnificent father.

Which reminded her. She'd better answer that letter from her Dad. It was getting close to the time when she'd need to ask for the Fall tuition money.

Chapter 21

MID-MORNING, two days later, just as Bronwen was about to start a complicated assay procedure, Felix limped over to where she was standing and asked her to step into his office. This was strange. She hadn't actually been there since her first day, more than six weeks ago.

"Can it wait? I'm ready to ..."

"I'd rather talk to you now."

Bronwen put down the stopwatch and followed Felix. Maybe her discovery had been a mirage. She was a fool after all.

He closed the door and asked her to sit down.

"Is something wrong? My work?" He shook his head no. Thank God. How bad could it be, then?

"Paulette? Did something happen to Paulette? Was there an accident?"

Felix rocked in place, his pipe clenched between his teeth and his hands clasped behind his back. "No," he said, "Paulette is fine."

The rocking accelerated until she thought he would tip over headfirst and wind up on the floor, spinning like a top, balanced on his beltbuckle.

"Bronwen ..." He took the pipe out of his mouth and put it on his desk. He ran his hands through his hair. She remembered this gesture later, the banality of it.

He looked down at her. "I received a telegram from California this morning. I'm very sorry to tell you that your father died last night."

She jumped to her feet. "No. That isn't true. No. No."

She began walking in a circle around his office. It was true, of course. The stilted letter, the photograph. He was dead. He had killed himself.

"No. No." She continued to walk around Felix, who stood helplessly in the middle of her mad circling.

"May I take you home? Had he been ill ...heart attack? Or is this ... I'm so sorry." He reached out and grabbed the voluminous sleeve of her borrowed labcoat, jerking her to a halt.

"It had to be suicide. I got a letter. It had to be." Her voice had become a toneless whisper.

Felix was stunned. He didn't know how to react. He tried to remember what people did in the soap operas his mother watched during those long Florida afternoons.

"Don't you want to go home for the rest of the day? I'd be glad to drive you."

He still gripped the cloth of her coat in his fist. He released it and she stuttered forward slightly.

"Yes. That would be good. That would be a very good idea."

Chapter 22

ONCE inside the door of their flat, Bronwen sat in the pleasant dimness of the living room trying to decide what to do first. She knew she should get up and call Eric. Maybe he would come home for lunch. Was it all right to be hungry if your father was dead? But as a matter of fact, she wasn't. And anyway, maybe he wasn't dead, either. Maybe if she got hungry, that would mean he hadn't died and the telegram was a bad joke. Her brain ached with all the possibilities. She sat in the cracked leather armchair, enjoying its cool touch against her arms and legs. Her eyes had almost closed when she heard a scraping at the front door and then voices. The ceiling light glared on and there in the hall stood Eric and a slender woman in a crisp white sundress and dark hair cut like Audrey Hepburn's. When Eric saw Bronwen sitting in the darkness, his eyes practically popped out onto the floor.

"Ah! Bronwen! Wow! Good! You're home! Wow! Talk about coincidences, I was just telling Gina about you, Gina, this is my roommate Bronwen. This is Gina Peruggi, Bron, remember I told you we have a new postdoc in the lab? She's looking for an apartment and she wanted to know what a typical place looks like... and how much she what are you doing home so early?"

Gina and Eric stood in the hallway, looking in her direction. Bronwen's heart was pounding so violently she was sure they could see it from across the room. She tossed out her sentences like knives.

"Felix drove me here. I got a telegram. My father died yesterday."

Gina murmured something, put her hand on Eric's shoulder, and was gone.

He rushed over to where Bronwen still sat rigidly in the decrepit leather chair.

"Babe, I'm so sorry."

"Are you screwing her?"

"Gina? She's years older than I am, give me some credit."

"She's gorgeous and she's probably brilliant. Are you, I repeat, screwing her?" She had expected an immediate denial, and Eric was definitely hedging.

"How can you give me the third degree like this when your father just died? Come on, let's get a sandwich or something and we'll talk later. I'm so glad you're here. Hey, chin up, c'mon now."

Bronwen stood up to follow him. If Eric didn't want her around, he would say so. All he had to do was say so. Just say the word.

She climbed up behind Eric and settled her pelvis in place, snugly up against the back of his. The motorcycle seat was warm, whether from the sun or Gina's flesh, who could say?

"All set? So, here we go. You never told me he was sick. What's the story?" She realized then that she didn't know a single detail. Things were happening too fast.

Chapter 23

SHE let Eric order her usual turkey on dark rye with extra tomato and mustard. Watching him get their Cokes out of the cooler up by the front counter, she felt strangely maternal. He looked so young; she felt so old. She looked down at her hands; chapped, the nails all different lengths. Hands of a lab rat. The place was quiet. They had never come here so early before.

A bad feeling started at her toes and began snaking up her legs, like the blue veins in an anatomy chart. Her father was dead. There was no more father.

"Okay. Lettuce for you, no mayo. We can split the fries." Eric finally sat down opposite her in the wooden booth and immediately took a huge bite of his sandwich. Considering the two possible topics before them—death and Gina—it was clear he would avoid conversation as long as he decently could. Bronwen decided to spare him the effort.

She pretended enthusiasm for the mound of food before her, and actually managed to bite off and begin chewing a good-sized mouthful. The problem was in swallowing. There already seemed to be a lump in her throat, and she could not imagine how she had ever swallowed in the past. She began to panic. Maybe if she dissolved it all in that universal solvent, Coca-Cola, she could survive this without anyone noticing. Mr. Cohen had once demonstrated for the eighth grade how a tooth left overnight in a glass of Coke would utterly disappear by the next day.

Eric was wolfing his sandwich and looking at his watch. She grabbed her glass, took a big swig, and waited. It worked. Still, the rest of her sandwich loomed in front of her.

Now the bad blue feeling was spreading through her ribs and down her arms into her fingertips. Her father was dead. The turkey meat was dead.

She pushed her plate to the side.

Eric met her eyes. "That's really too bad about your Dad." Eric had never met her father. She decided not to tell him her suicide theory; it wasn't any of his business.

"Have you talked to your Mom yet?" Bronwen shook her head. Of course, she would have to tell her mother. None of the California relatives knew how to reach her. Maybe Bronwen would even go down to Manhattan for the weekend and see her.

113

She cleared her throat. "Are you going right back to the lab?" Eric nodded, his mouth too full to speak.

"Then I might hang around the Square for a bit and go to a bookstore or something. I don't feel like being in the apartment right now."

Released, Eric rose abruptly and gave her a quick peck on the forehead. So anxious was he to go that he left half of his dill pickle and almost all of his cole slaw uneaten. He gave her a jaunty wave as the BMW rolled past the window where she was sitting.

If she went to New York for the weekend it would definitely leave the coast clear for Gina. There was no way Bronwen and Eric could both go. Her mother's studio apartment was tiny, and they couldn't afford to stay in a hotel. She would have to go alone and take her chances with the Italian bombshell.

The long walk to Harvard Square calmed her nerves somewhat, and gave her a purpose. Before returning to the empty flat to make the unavoidable call to her mother in New York, she would buy a copy of Rilke's *Letters To A Young Poet*. That promised to be easier going than *The Notebooks of Malte Laurids Brigge*. The bookstore clerk had never heard of this but Bronwen had discovered it on Eric's bookshelf the week before. He, in turn, had inherited it from the previous occupant of the flat—or so he claimed. Bronwen wondered now if a female of Gina's ilk had left it there the preceding winter. The pages gave off faint whiffs of a vaguely European cologne, 7-11 Gesundheitwasser perhaps. In any case, she would definitely need something to read on the bus trip and Rilke's story of a young Danish nobleman losing his marbles in the disease-ridden slums of Paris was definitely not the ticket. Not now.

Her brain was beginning to short circuit, not knowing whether to go into sad or mad mode. The result was an unfamiliar numbness.

As she passed the windows of inexpensive Chinese restaurants and clothing boutiques, bookshops and ice cream parlors, she felt entombed in a private world of pain and suffering while the rest of Cambridge went about its usual pursuit of summery pleasures. So self-absorbed was she that she failed to notice Felix emerging from Baskin-Robbins, bearing a torch of triple-dip pistachio with chocolate sprinkles. He started to wave, then suppressed the gesture when he saw the dull expression on her face. He stepped back into the doorway and let her pass by. In a moment, he popped out again and began to trail her, holding his cone high so he could lick it without taking his eyes off the thick blanket of her hair as she moved steadily forward among the lunchtime crowd.

When Bronwen entered Grolier's, the middle-aged clerk (the owner?) sitting on a high wooden stool by the cash register glanced up and then back down at his book, snap judgment complete in a blink. He probably figured she'd wandered into the wrong place and would be gone in a few moments.

Bronwen lingered shyly by the door until she got her bearings. This was only her second time inside Cambridge's oldest and most prestigious used bookstore. All around her were unfamiliar treasures, laid out in heaps on long tables or piled on sagging bookshelves. The large, bright room was roughly square, with wide plate glass windows that fronted on the street and allowed passersby a clear view of the interior. Most of the books were crammed in cases against the walls, while the owner's special favorites were displayed face up on the long tables, an all-you-can-read-buffet. Not very efficient use of space, but a welcome visual relief from the crowded aisles of the chain bookstores closer to the center of the Square.

In one corner was a lumpy green brocade armchair with the stuffing beginning to extrude. It was occupied by a young man sporting a fitful growth of beard, wearing a black t-shirt and sandals. He was rather ostentatiously holding a heavy volume on his lap and reciting one of its pages softly to himself. If Bronwen squinted she could make out the name W.B. Yeats in white on a blue dustjacket.

Trying not to let her footsteps echo too loudly on the bare wooden floorboards, Bronwen nervously approached the clerk. She was looking directly at the bald spot on his forward-tilted head when she coughed.

"Yes?" His head jerked upright. "And, please, for pity's sake, don't creep up on a person like that." Bronwen was now close enough to see that he had been reading Madame Bovary. In French.

"Do you have a ..."

"No, we don't have a Restroom. Not even for customers."

"That's not what I wanted to ...I was wondering if you have ..." In mid-sentence, she panicked. She wanted to escape, fast. Black t-shirt in the corner had lowered his book and was glaring at her.

"... if you have Robert Lowell's *LIFE STUDIES*," she finished, reading the first dustjacket that came into focus. The clerk was shocked, but recovered fast, revealing nicotine-stained teeth in an unexpectedly sweet smile. "Why, yes, we do. An estate purchase just came in, as a matter of fact."

He swiveled his rotund body around and plucked a slender volume from the top of the open cardboard carton sitting on a huge cluttered desk just behind him.

"A fan, are you?"

"I want to be ... his honesty attracts me. And his language. But sometimes he's so private ..."

"I know. And so unpredictable. Uneven. But you'll like this one. It's a real change of pace. A breakthrough. And what luck to have a First Edition! Do you need anything else? More Lowell?"

He lifted himself off the stool and began to bustle about, all his senses alert to the possibility of the first real sale of the week.

"Well ..." She timidly mentioned Rilke.

"Christ yes, we're up to our yin-yangs in Rilke ... Comparative Lit major, are you?" Before she knew it, he had stacked four more books on his counter, all smelling of fresh ink. She was going to have to write a cheque. The total was way over her budget, but they were as irresistible as boxes of candy.

Now black t-shirt was, there was no denying it, actively scowling in her direction.

She took out her wallet. Alarm bells were beginning to sound deep down in her midbrain. "No, actually, chemistry is ..."

Black t-shirt stood up in his corner. For a moment, she thought he might hurl the heavy collected Yeats at her head.

"Chemistry! CHEM-IS-TRY! You won't understand Robert Lowell! Don't sell her those books! She won't understand a word! Literal-minded scientist snob! I had a Physics teacher in high school who told me I was stupid! Failed me! HE was the stupid one! Robert Lowell! Ha!" As suddenly as he had begun, he sat down and resumed reading.

Bronwen stood stock-still, mortified to the tips of every hair on her head. Sweat dripped down her back and chafed at the waistband of her jeans.

"Don't mind him. That's just Richard. He's harmless. You come back again and tell me how you liked these books. Promise? And I took 10% off for quantity." He gave her the books in a sturdy dark blue bag emblazoned with the shop's logo in gold lettering, then turned back to Emma Bovary. Bronwen was ready now, fortified by her purchase. No more excuses: time to call her mother.

Outside, Felix was getting restless and he also needed to pee. He had seen the pantomime performance of black t-shirt and assumed a friend of Bronwen's was greeting her. He felt a stab of nostalgia for the days when he, too, had hung out in bookstores hoping to meet a pretty girl. Now look at him. What was he doing here, anyway?

He'd wait a couple more minutes and then he'd give up and go to a movie. An air-conditioned movie, maybe that Doris Day thing at the Square.

She was coming his way! As best he could, he flattened himself along the wall by the entrance, so that when Bronwen emerged, the door banged hard against the soles of his shoes. They looked at each other through the panes of glass in the door.

It was Felix! He was going to tell her the telegram was a bad joke, or a mistake, that really Inge was the intended recipient, it was Inge's elderly father in Israel who had keeled over ....

Bronwen closed the door to the shop and beamed at the figure of her supervisor who had come to turn back the clock, to put her world back together.

"Felix! How did you find me? Do you have some good news? It was a mix-up, wasn't it?"

Only now did he realize the gravity of his mistake in following her. If ever he had hated himself, he hated himself at this moment.

"No ... I was kind of concerned, that's all. I saw you walking ... and I thought you might like to talk. Or something. How about getting some donuts and going down to the river?" He wanted to die. He was a fool, a jerk, a muddleheaded-moron. An asshole.

The dull expression settled back over her features. She was still the daughter of a dead, dead father. A really dead dad. It was all she could do not to laugh in Felix's face. That would be terrible. He was trying so hard to be nice.

She nodded yes. " But not for too long... I have to go back and call my mother. I don't even know if she's heard yet." Noticing Felix's puzzled look, she continued talking as they made their way to Dunkin' Donuts. "They've been divorced for years. She lives by herself in Manhattan and doesn't keep in touch with the California branch of the family."

"If anything like this happened in my clan, you'd have 44 people on the phone for the next eighteen hours." Felix stopped, hoping he hadn't insulted her in some way. For the first time in his life, he wished for the gift of tact.

"Well, ours isn't exactly a typical WASP family, either. But that's a whole other story."

He held the door open for her, and they entered the air-conditioned bliss of the bakery. The aroma of maple icing mixed with the glorious fumes of hot shortening and powdered sugar. Not a bagel in sight, only soft white dough in a thousand disguises. The first bite into a fresh apple fritter was like sex—always a shockingly delicious surprise, always new. For Felix, women and doughnuts were proof that some kind of benevolent intelligence was responsible for the universe as he knew it.

"Okay. Lemon creme jelly doughnut you, glazed maple bar me. Iced tea you, milk me. Mazeltov!" Felix crumpled the bakery bag in one fist and took a huge bite of the warm pastry. He raised his milk carton in her direction and sipped energetically through his straw, nearly emptying the container in one go. Sugar was galloping through his veins, but he felt something else too. Ashamed, he tried to push the feeling away, but he couldn't help it. Bronwen's father was dead, but the result was that he and she were sitting on the grass, with a cloudless blue sky above and the Charles River lapping almost at their feet, sweet rotting aquatic weeds and grasses lifted by the swells rolling from the hulls of Harvard skiffs gliding by in the far distance. He glanced over and saw that she was lying on her back, oblivious to him, one arm thrown over her eyes. Her underarm was hairless and faintly frosted with the white glaze of her deodorant.

There must be something he could do.
Then it occurred to him.

"Do you know Caleb O'Donnell? I think he's going to New

York this weekend. He could give you a ride to your mother's. If you were planning to go, I mean. And you don't need to come into the lab until you're ready, you know..." He was on his stomach now, tossing around loose clumps of grass, inhaling their scent. The slope had recently been mowed. Everything was perfect. He had not been so happy for years.

Bronwen sat up, a hand shading her eyes. "I want to. I want to do that enzyme series we talked about. But not tomorrow."

Now she was standing, a black silhouette looming over him.

"Felix, thanks for this, but I really have to go and call her now. My mom."

She was brushing loose grass off the seat of her white jeans. There would be permanent dark green stains on the rear. Would she look at them and remember this day, remember sitting here with him? He hauled himself to his feet, collecting bits of sticky wax paper and slowly stuffing them into the crumpled Dunkin' Donuts bag.

"Did I ever tell you my theory of the Repressor Gene?" Felix had pulled himself together and plunged back into being Felix. "I'm writing a grant about it right now. Some French scientists think that the Lambda virus makes a substance that turns its bacterial host's DNA off and lets the virus go wild. They don't know if it's large or small, or if it's DNA or a protein—but it's the Holy Grail of molecular biology right now and I want to be the one to find it."

Felix glanced sideways at Bronwen. She seemed to be listening. "The incredible thing is that it could serve as a model for how embryonic development occurs—for turning DNA on and off in different genes as the different tissues and organs of a fetus take shape. But to study it in such a humble setting as the common intestinal bacterium—it's diabolically brilliant." Felix hoped he was distracting her with his self-important babble.

They meandered back to Felix's VW, Bronwen clutching her heavy bundle of books, Felix waving his hands in the air as he described the scheme he would employ to isolate and purify the Repressor.

Bronwen didn't have the heart to tell him that Eric and his group were currently doing similar experiments and that a draft of a manuscript was already in progress. She played dumb and opened her eyes wide as Felix rattled forth justifications for his approach to the problem.

It really was none of her business. She had to save her energy for the phone call. And then there was the question of the trip home. If there was a free ride available, she could hardly avoid going. It was the least she could do.

Anyway, she needed to talk to someone who knew her. Felix, even at his most benign, wasn't family.

And Eric ... well, Eric was just Eric.

Chapter 24

CALEB was wearing the only outfit she'd ever seen him in—white shirt, no tie, top button buttoned, faded Levi's and a black suit jacket of some shiny gabardine-like fabric that was at least one size too small. This get-up was not in itself so outrageous, except that all the other males in the lab wore the standard uniform of blue or white oxford-cloth shirt and army-issue chinos, with the occasional daring flash of knee by a reckless Bermuda shorts wearer. It wasn't his uniqueness that bothered Bronwen, it was just that the few times she'd seen him, in a seminar or in the hallway, he seemed so ...calculating, somehow.

Yes, she had to admit it, everything about Caleb bothered Bronwen. The more she thought about it, the more she regretted accepting his offer of a ride to Manhattan for the weekend. She should have just gone to the bus station and hopped on the Friday morning commuter special.

It was too late now. Her mother was expecting her and Bronwen didn't feel comfortable about postponing the visit. The occasion was going to be awkward enough, talking about the death of her father with the woman who'd hardly spoken to him since their divorce and hadn't even seen him after his move to find the Good Life in Southern California. But there was no one else anywhere near Bronwen this summer who had known her father, and she felt compelled to mark his death by at least reminiscing about him, since she couldn't afford to fly West for the funeral. If there was even going to be a funeral.

Now here was Caleb in the flesh, walking towards her and reaching over for her overnight bag. She caught a whiff of stale cigarette smoke and a hint of garlic. Oh my God, this was going to be an ordeal.

"Sorry about your old man. I heard ... from Felix. Tough break."

She was furious. How dare virtual strangers discuss her personal life. She searched her empty head for a cutting remark but before she could say anything, she realized that he had simply continued his trajectory and was now sitting behind the wheel of his ridiculous hump-backed red Volvo. "You coming, or am I taking just your suitcase to New York?"

She slid resentfully in beside him and was astonished to see how his body filled the car. His arms and legs were long and lean, storklike. Eric really was a small person. Caleb's knees poked out from jagged holes in his faded Levi's. She fought an impulse to snigger when she realized the unintended impression of his get-up was that of an overgrown kid trying to squeeze one more Halloween out of his vanishing childhood. Caleb would make a perfect Scarecrow to Judy Garland's Dorothy.

On the dashboard was glued a small white label, and a neat inscription in purple ink that read, "He who despises himself esteems himself as a self-despiser"... Nietzsche.

Caleb shifted into gear and pulled away from the curb. He noticed her reading the quote and he looked at the copy of *Letters to a Young Poet* lying half-concealed in her lap. "So, Rilke," he said. "Well, there's a German for everyone, I guess."

Bronwen remained quiet. She was not going to rise to any nihilist bait. In any case, she had read so little of the actual contents of her book that she was by no means prepared to discuss even a single page of it.

It was going to be a very long ride.

They drove for half an hour in a silence punctuated by occasional bursts of humming from Caleb. She caught a phrase that sounded like "No, no, it ain't me, Babe, it ain't me you're looking for." You've got that right, she thought.

He seemed to be a good driver, though, shifting easily and smoothly in the stop-and-go traffic as they made their escape from Boston. It was a relief to be encased in glass and metal, with room to stretch her legs out, after all the frenzied, jerky motorcycle jaunts with Eric. Bronwen began to breathe more deeply, and even to look forward to seeing Katherine. It had been more than a year since she had seen her mother, with only 2 or 3 postcards to connect them. This time, at least, they would have a subject other than Bronwen's Life to discuss.

"Ever heard of a folk singer—well, sort of a folkie— named Bobby Dylan? Plays in Cambridge sometimes." Caleb kept his eyes on the road as he spoke.

"No ... but we don't go to coffee houses or folk clubs much."

"Is that the royal We?"

"My boyfriend ...and his friends."

"Oh, right. You're with Eric what's-his-ass, right? Harvard grad student? Biology? That was my first choice, actually."

"Yes." Again, that feeling that he knew everything about her, that she was a chloroformed moth pinned to a wax display slab. There really was no privacy in the overlapping science circles. She knew that Caleb was a second year grad student at Ronstein, although Felix had told her it was doubtful that he would pass his qualifying exam this Fall. Bright enough, but too contrary. Just wouldn't take direction from any of his professors. Felix spoke highly of Caleb in private, but he had little enough influence to spare, even for a kindred spirit. His own nose was barely above water.

Caleb continued. "My mom claims that Harvard has a quota, and that's why I didn't get in, but that's what moms are for. False reassurances all the way. You get along with your old lady?"

Bronwen couldn't stand his slang, but at least he was trying to be friendly, so she concealed her irritation. She considered his question, flipping the paperback Rilke volume nervously in her lap, face up, face down. Since her father's death, she carried it everywhere with her.

"We have a sort of negotiated truce, I guess. She's stopped asking me if there's a chaperone along on my camping trips, and I've stopped asking her for spending money. She's accepted the fact that I'm not going to be an English major. For a long time she was hoping I'd follow in her footsteps and be a failed writer. Thanks but no thanks."

"Wow, lady, you sound bitter ... Sonuvabitch! Sorry about that, truck drivers around here are the worst. No, really, is that why you're becoming a lab rat? To annoy your mother? I always thought it was the mighty Eric's positive influence."

"Jesus Christ, I was interested in genetics before I even met Eric, why does everyone ..." Her voice trailed off unconvincingly. It was that old bullshit again.

Caleb reached over and touched her knee lightly. "I sit corrected. Let's drop it, okay? What are you doing when we get into the city? I've got the use of a friend's walk-up on Bleecker Street for the whole weekend and he always has the best hoard of Italian goodies in town." He glanced over at the still angry Bronwen.

"I could make amends by rustling up the best clams in white sauce you've ever ingested, then drop you into your loving mother's lap. C'mon, don't make me flagellate myself all weekend because I was rude and presumptious once. And I'll wager that I'm better in the kitchen than your Mom."

Bronwen finally laughed. "How did you guess she's a lousy cook?"

"Psychic, of course. One of my many hidden talents. The others remain to be revealed." He began humming again. In spite of herself, she began sneaking little sideways glances at him from the corner of her left eye.

"Hey, Bronwen buddy, hand me that jug of wine from behind my seat, will you? It's sticking out of the Bloomingdale's shopping bag."

"Should you be ..."

"One or two little sips won't hurt. Just to get a tad of a buzz on. We have to get acquainted before we eat together, don't we?"

Finally they were there, endlessly looking for a parking place. Bronwen's limbs felt long and supple, suffused with a warm glow. Caleb and she, entirely against her better judgment, had actually finished the Chianti. They seemed to have sprouted a web of connectedness with each other. They trudged, tittering, up the four flights, Caleb insisting that they bring her overnight bag so it wouldn't get stolen from the car. His enormous feet, in scuffed shapeless black shoes, appeared and disappeared at eye level as she lagged behind him, panting and dizzy from the exertion and the alcohol.

At the top landing, she admired his tapered fingers as he tried to fit the key into the battered deadbolt lock.

She wanted to reach up and stroke the back of his neck, hidden under the thick cluster of reddish-brown curls. He was half-Irish on his father's side, she had learned. That explained the pale skin and the generous sprinkling of freckles over his nose and high cheekbones. In profile in the dim hallway, he reminded her of the fur-hatted minor Renaissance nobleman that was one of her favorite postcards from the Metropolitan. And he was so tall.

She stood behind him, trying to think clearly. Trying to think at all. Her breasts seemed to be magnetically pulling her towards his shoulder blades, protruding from the back of his shabby jacket.

When the door finally popped open, he fell forward, almost losing his balance for a moment. Bronwen hesitated at the threshold. She caught a glimpse of a bathtub next to the kitchen sink. Even from the hallway, the flat reeked of curry powder and olive oil.

He turned around and looked down at her. "Are you on the Pill?"

She nodded.

"Call your mother and tell her you were delayed. Please. Let's just have this one night. Please. No one will ever know. You have my word. Please."

He made no move to touch her.

Her body flamed with the most intense desire she had ever known. She wouldn't be surprised if he told her smoke was billowing from the top of her head.

She sleepwalked to the phone in the kitchen and dialed.

Behind her, Caleb was methodically snapping the locks into place.

Chapter 25

HIS arms enfolded her. The slightly chapped mouth brushed across her forehead, moving across eyes to cheek, then soft, soft ....

"Like some more coffee, sweetie? Macaroons? We can have lunch whenever you say."

Katherine, more used to the role of exotic Bohemian than mother, hovered near Bronwen's cup, balanced on one of the wide arms of the old blue armchair. "Just say when."

Caleb's face vanished, but the feel of his body pressed tightly up against hers stayed with Bronwen. His hands unbuttoned her blouse again and again.

She sat cross-legged and tried to look appropriately solemn and attentive as her mother puttered about, postponing the inevitable moment when they would have to acknowledge the death of a man whose life had been essentially a mystery to both of them. Bronwen was ready to escape, to sleep, to dream of Caleb, but Katherine was not about to give up on her captive audience. Now that her daughter was sitting here in front of her house, she would suck every drop of meaning and information out of these precious two days. Whatever she gleaned was going to have to last her over the winter, maybe even two winters.

At times like this, Bronwen felt like the harpooned seal at an Eskimo feast. Worst of all, the more eager her mother was to glean details of her life, the more stubbornly reticent Bronwen became. She hadn't even decided whether or not to relate the news about her unexpected luck in discovering the enzyme last week. It just seemed like Katherine always wanted to take credit somehow for every good thing that happened to Bronwen. And not, of course, for any of the bad. It wasn't fair.

And now that a really bad thing had happened, neither of them knew how to begin talking about it. Bronwen directed her gaze inward, away from Katherine's stretchy chartreuse tube top, worn without a bra (she'd been doing this since the 1950's) and long, wrinkled skirt that looked like a curtain from a Florida motel. It was that textured, fake linen-y material and had a repeating parrot motif.

"No more coffee, Mom, thanks. By the way, is that skirt an actual curtain?"

"Yes, isn't it fabulous? Don't you love it?" Her mother twirled coquettishly, first being careful to bend over and flick the ash off her cigarette into her empty coffee cup. Katherine fooled herself into believing she didn't smoke so heavily by never having a proper ashtray. "I got the set for two bucks at the Salvation Army on Seventy-third and West End Avenue. And I'm going to make a shawl out of the other panel."

"On you, it's perfect." Bronwen was fighting to keep her eyes open. Her thoughts drifted, and Caleb returned.

Keeping his eyes level with hers, without looking down, Caleb was unzipping her jeans, very slowly, as he kissed her exposed collar bones. First one, then the other. She opened her eyes wider and kept her gaze directed towards Katherine.

"Well." Her mother plopped down on the daybed and leaned back. "I guess it's up to me to start. It wasn't your fault in any way. You know that."

"Fault? What do you mean?" Here comes the hook. Bronwen braced herself.

"He was a difficult man. Obviously. I never wanted to criticize him after we divorced. He was your father, after all, and I never did have a need to play those kinds of games. And to tell you the honest truth, I wasn't that surprised. He was *always* threatening to kill himself."

Bronwen felt the old anger surging back, began to loathe the sight of her mother's sagging breasts in the tube top, hated her too bright lipstick and the mascara that always seemed to smear within minutes of being applied.

A skinny 12-year-old, coming home with a load of books and hours of homework, Bronwen had opened the door to their two-room hotel "suite" on West Eighth Street in the Village to find Katherine in bed with Tony, the ten-years-younger actor her mother had been dating. Bronwen had stomped into the bathroom, crying, and refused to open the door. "Tramp!" she shouted to the rattling doorknob. "Tramp!"

When Bronwen finally opened the door, her mother slumped to the floor, crying and asking her forgiveness. Bronwen, her nose red from blowing it with toilet paper, could only stare down in misery at the small gold safety pin holding Katherine's ivory satin strap to the back of her slip. They sent out for Chinese food and never discussed the incident again.

Katherine coughed and lit another cigarette. "But I never actually thought he'd do it. I mean, forgive me, but it shows he had some balls at the end, anyway. Pardon my French." She inhaled and then blew a slow stream of smoke into the room. The familiar smell of Katherine's Pall Malls, the crimson package with the heraldic lions rearing up, put Bronwen into a kind of comfortable stupor. It was like their family crest; she was Home. Not that it was a place she could ever bring Eric. He wouldn't understand, would find it, at best, bizarre. For Bronwen there was this consolation: if you could only escape, there was no place to go but up.

"Moth-er! That was a terrible thing to say."

"I know. But I only meant to emphasize that you weren't responsible for Roger screwing up his life. And, guess what?" She took a long drag and exhaled with a little explosion of coughs. "I wasn't either."

Bronwen shifted in her chair. "I never said you were."

She took a sip of the dreadful instant Nescafe cooling in her cup. Here we go again.

Weren't they supposed to be honoring their dead? She tried to think of something to say about her father. Something nice that wouldn't offend her mother. This whole business was a lot trickier than she had anticipated, especially considering the almost total lack of sleep she had gotten last night.

Last night. Last night Caleb was nibbling at Bronwen's breast, taking her right nipple into his mouth. He was on his knees between her legs, hands on her waist; she, sitting on a stranger's bed with her hands gripping that curly red hair. Eric had never bothered much with nipples.

"Honey, you've been mad at me for sixteen years because I divorced your dad. Let's be frank. Isn't that why you're here?"

"I don't know why I'm here." Bronwen fought to keep control of her voice. "I thought you invited me so we could trade funny little anecdotes and stuff, not so you could tell me for the millioneth time how you aren't perfect and you did your best and someday I'll understand and if I only knew what it was like to have your mother die when you were ten years old ... I DON'T WANT TO HEAR THAT CRAP ANYMORE! I'M VERY SORRY ABOUT YOUR MOTHER AND EVERYTHING BUT I WANT TO TALK ABOUT MY FATHER! CAN'T YOU EVER THINK ABOUT ANYONE BUT YOURSELF?"

Silence. The sound of the elevator gate creaking in the outside hall. Footsteps, a key turning a lock, a distant door opening and closing. Silence.

Bronwen looked over at Katherine, who was staring vacantly in front of her.

"Mom?"

"Toasters. We always had toasters, and irons. He sold thermostats, you know. Traveled all over the Northeast. An engineering degree from Purdue, and he sells thermostats.

And he was a pretty good cook. Always said that the great chefs were men. He never let me forget that."

"Mom. It's alright."

"He always made sure your shoes fit. It was an obsession. Those Oxfords every year. Until you got those damn white bucks. Which, incidentally, I wound up polishing half the time. And the swimming. Well, you know about that. He could do the most beautiful jackknife you ever saw. At his age! But I never could stand the chlorine in those hotel health clubs. The man looked good in a trench coat, I'll give him that. Did he ever tell you he was a reporter for a while, just before we met?"

"Mother ..."

"And talk about cuff links. You must have given him 10 or 12 sets. Father's Day, birthdays, it adds up. Why did cuff links ever become obsolete? There was one pair, tiger's eye agates, I think ...they must have cost ..."

"Mother, stop, please."

Katherine leaned forward from her awkward position on the daybed. "I once loved him. We both wanted to have the baby that turned out to be you. For your sake, I'm sorry he died the way he did. Shall we call a truce? For today, anyway?"

Bronwen nodded. He was really dead. Like the stiff little sparrow they had once buried under an elm in Washington

Square Park. At this very moment, they might be lowering him into the ground of the Naval Cemetery in Santa Barbara.

"And now," Katherine proclaimed as she lumbered clumsily off the bed, "I, a mere female cook, shall make a Spanish omelet for my brilliant daughter. How is your summer job working out? Are you still seeing Eric what's-his-name? Would you dice some green pepper for me? Not too small, about like that."

Bronwen stood up. This was the moment when she should be going over to give her mother a hug. But she couldn't. She just could not.

Caleb moved aside, out of the picture, out of her brain. The path to Katherine was unimpeded. Still, she couldn't do it. With a tight smile on her face, Bronwen walked over to the small cutting board on the pink formica counter of the Pullman kitchenette.

Katherine, a cigarette drooping from one side of her mouth, opened the frig and took out a carton of eggs. Humming "Some Enchanted Evening," she began to break eggs into a Pyrex mixing bowl.

Back to back, Bronwen and Katherine worked, cracking and chopping. Bronwen fiercely willed Caleb's return, but it was no go. She and her mother would have to get through the day on their own. At that instant Bronwen realized she had left her contraceptive Pillpak back on the top of the bureau in her bedroom in Boston.

The shock made her narrowly miss cutting off the tip of her thumb. She would not be able to take a Pill for two more days.

Chapter 26

KATHERINE left for work in a cloud of White Lilac talcum powder and Chanel No.5, leaving behind a note reminding Bronwen to meet her at 5:30 for egg foo yung at their favorite Chinese place in the Village and then the first showing of *Bicycle Thief*. It was a double feature with *The Rose Tattoo* but if that was too much for one evening they could just go for ice cream and come home. As soon as she left, Bronwen was wide awake and after reading the note began to pace the hall restlessly in her underwear. She flopped in the sagging armchair with the scarlet hibiscus slipcover and picked up the copy of Colette's *Cheri* that lay on the cluttered coffee table. She flipped the pages without being able to focus. It didn't seem possible that she could stay here all day and another night. She'd better just check the bus schedule and leave on her own. She was going to pretend the incident with Caleb had never happened. She hadn't been in her right mind, that's all.

The insistent ringing of the phone broke through the dull surface of her mind. Maybe there was a change of plans for tonight. And anyway, she should tell her mother she was leaving early and not just sneak away.

"Hello? Yes, this is Bronwen. Felix?"

Motorcycle accident, Eric, blood? Her father alive, the telegram a practical joke?

"Is everything o.k.? Oh...good." She sat down among the dusty folds of hibiscus and listened for his meaning. Her nerves were on edge at the hint of anything wrong. Her brain heard each word separately and distinctly. He wanted to come by her mother's house. He was in New York. She agreed, assuming he was going to bring some kind of potted lily for her mother. Strange for him to be here, though. Had he told her he would be coming to New York?

Bronwen pulled on her black cotton tank dress and brushed her hair. She pulled it back in a low pony-tail and found an old black velvet ribbon on her mother's dresser. Using a damp sponge to blot off old powder smudges, she freshened it up and tied it over the rubber band securing her hair. Make-upless and barefoot, she roamed around, munching on a carrot stick. She jumped when she heard the hall buzzer. She returned the buzz, and then waited for the sound of the familiar heavy steps. There was a long silence when the footsteps stopped, and she opened the peephole, beginning to doubt that it was Felix.

It was him, alright, staring at his shoes and panting. He was holding a large bunch of roses. Not very funereal, but thoughtful. She felt more cheerful already. After he left, maybe she'd go down to her old stomping grounds in the Village. Go by the apartment building where her father used to live. Yeah, and maybe leave a rose in the lobby behind the potted ferns. Then she'd browse around and look for new sandals before meeting her mother for dinner. The hollow, cold sensation that had invaded her chest since her father's death began to ease for the first time. She finished undoing the last of the complicated door locks, inhaled deeply and opened the door.

Perspiration was running down Felix's temples and trickling down his cheeks onto his limp collar. "Here. For you. I am, really, very sorry."

"Thank you, that's very, but you didn't need to ... I didn't know you were going to be in New York. Do you want a cup of instant coffee? That's all my mother has." Bronwen backed into the room slightly. Felix was staring at her with a weird fixed expression. Suddenly he was on the floor, his fingers gripping her ankles.

Without looking up, he spoke, rapidly and disjointedly. "I hate myself for doing this, I'm sorry, but I have to tell you. I have to. And live with the consequences. I love you. I'm crazy for you. I can't keep it to myself any longer. Just tell me you don't hate me."

Bronwen stood just inside the doorway, pinned to the spot by his deathgrip on her ankles. A thorn from one of the rose stems was digging into her palm. This must be a dream. This couldn't be happening to her. "You didn't say this, Felix. You don't mean it. And you know that Eric is the one ..."

"I do mean it. And you know he doesn't love you the way I do ... he's in love with himself. I can wait for you to graduate, I can ..."

Bronwen felt sick to her stomach. She looked down and saw the sweat stains spreading in a line down his back. "Felix, I'm going to ask you to go now. This never happened. I will never tell anybody. You have to go now. Thank you for the roses. Take your hands away from my legs."

He released his grip, but as he drew his fingers away, he stroked the sides of her bare feet very delicately with the tips of his fingers, shuddered, and backed out into the hall, his rear end sticking up and his face still directed at the floor. He put his face in his hands and stayed there. The skin on her feet tingled, confusing her for a moment. Then, very gently, Bronwen closed the door until the lock clicked into place.

She turned and ran to the bathroom, dropping the roses on the kitchen floor as she went. She closed the door and sat trembling on the closed toilet seat. It felt like another death.

Chapter 27

AFTER a long time had passed, maybe an hour, Bronwen stood up. She should pull herself together. This might be her last day in New York for years.

She had about three hours before she was due to meet Katherine at the 8th Street Playhouse, the miniscule showcase for artsy foreign films a block from where they used to live in the Village. Each of her parents had dragged her there on rainy Sunday afternoons to squirm through grainy subtitled movies ever since she could remember. Her mother had recently scored the coup of getting the part-time evening job of serving espresso in their lobby, handing out tiny white cups with a twist of lemon floating on the surface of the dark brew. The only money she made was whatever tips people left, but it gave her a chance to "study" the films for free. (Bronwen suspected that mandatory visits to the manager's private office in back might also be part of the job description, but she kept these thoughts to herself.)

Tonight Katherine was off-duty, but her boss was letting her take Bronwen to the double bill at no charge. They were to meet in the lobby around five. Plenty of time to drift around the Village a bit.

She splashed cold water on her face and slipped into her sandals. It would be pleasant to walk on streets where nobody knew her by sight anymore. A long, anonymous and uneventful week. Slinging her ink-blotched burgundy leather shoulder bag over her head and across her back, she was out the door, actually beginning to look forward to this private encounter with the city of her birth.

Before she reached the elevator, she turned around and went back to get a single rose from the bunch that Felix (oh God Felix why did you do it) had brought. She would carry out her plan to leave a flower as a tribute to her father. The rest of the bunch she stuck in cold water in a battered aluminum coffeepot that hadn't been used for years.

When she emerged from the Sheridan Square subway station, she was surprised to find herself literally unable to walk directly towards her father's last apartment. She would need to sneak up on it more gradually.

As Bronwen hesitated, a tall woman with short black hair, wearing paint-spattered jeans and carrying a large gray artist's portfolio, pushed past her. It was Gina, rushing to meet Eric! Drenched in paranoia, Bronwen began following the woman—but no, her nose was larger and her breasts smaller than her Boston look-alike. She was also much too tall. And then Bronwen realized she was on West 11th Street, and here was the garden duplex her father had sublet that summer she had the terrible case of whooping cough. It wasn't far from the apartment where she and her mother lived, on Perry Street, but what a difference, she now saw.

Eleventh Street was for people who had made it, or tourists with money to spend in fancy little steakhouses with awnings and steps down into their cozy interiors. It had houses with freshly painted iron grillwork balconies, and brass letterflaps and red geraniums in windowboxes and sparkly clean windows through which you could see fireplaces and bookshelves to the ceiling and black and white etchings and *New Yorkers* on coffee tables and way at the back the green of the gardens. Oh, yes, definitely an adult world, unlike the territory of Perry Street, just three blocks west. Bronwen passed St. Vincent's hospital and stopped at the corner of Perry and Seventh Avenue.

Perry Street, now lush with summer foliage, had been kids' territory, summer and winter. Bronwen and her cronies had dominated the landscape night and day and knew every spit-smeared inch of it, the guy in the cellar who sold blocks of ice and sacks of coal, the penny candy store with the 40 watt light bulb hanging over stale chocolate-covered caramels that could break your teeth, the grandmothers stationed in every front window, peering through the peeling black and orange fire escapes at the granddaughers and their dolls snugly ensconced at the tops of the damp basement stairs that led down to each Super's subterranean dwelling. (Bronwen knew she had lost major points for having neither a living grandmother nor a resident father.) Her old front stoop was still guarded by the winged twin gryphons, cast iron painted glossy black, their forelegs extended and still grasping softball-sized globes in their four- inch-long shining black talons. Those steps were inviolate territory, but control over one's sidewalk frontage was a constantly challenged prerogative: It's a free country, I can stand here if I want to! The penalty for such a challenge was high; Bronwen had chalked, secretly at night: ROSES ARE RED, HORSES ARE TAN, BERNICE BELTON'S FACE IS LIKE A FRYING PAN! in two-foot high letters on the asphalt in front of the offender's building. But they were recent Irish, not shy and oh God the next day Bernice's brother called Bronwen out to her stoop and told her if she ever did anything like that again he'd throw her down the *frigging* cellar stairs, and no one had ever said *frigging* to her before, it sounded much worse than *fucking*, which she *had* heard, so that was the end of Fridays with Bernice and the only television set Bronwen had access to, the end of potato chips and Cokes with ice cubes and running across the street after the 9:00 science fiction hour, and seeing their St. Christopher's medal up by the kitchen door, which they touched when they went out so they wouldn't get run over. Later Bernice got ringworm in spite of St. C.; Bronwen didn't know this until someone dared her to pull off the long woolen stocking cap Bernice wore night and day and there she was BALD right in front of everyone. Her hair, straight like Buster Brown's beforehand, grew in curly afterwards, so it was O.K.; in fact, Bronwen prayed for years that she would get ringworm too but never did, only lice. (To whom or what she prayed was not clear, but pray she did: for curly hair, snow, a puppy, smaller feet and her parents to get married again. Or, second choice, for Roy Rogers to die and her father to marry Dale Evans. This last wish she knew was vaguely evil but she couldn't help it.)

Now Bronwen stared—an Antique Emporium had replaced the Svensson's, whose grocery store had a tiled floor that was sprinkled with fresh sawdust every day, and a butcher in a white apron who was married to the lady who served you. She had a braid wound around her head and looked exactly like the mother in *I Remember Mama*, Bronwen's favorite program next to the science fiction. And just about as realistic, compared to her own life.

Everyone did their shopping there, and voted for Miss Rheingold every year, everyone except the people who lived in the houses on the corner near 7th Avenue, the ones that had thick straw mats in vestibules, in the corners of which Bronwen et al. used to relieve themselves on hot summer nights during hide 'n' seek games when they didn't go home because if they ran in and out ONE MORE TIME they'd have to STAY in; she wondered what those people thought, coming home with their little packages of freshly ground espresso beans and coffee cake from Sutter's (dripping with vanilla icing and pecans) and maybe a bottle of brandy to tide them over another Saturday night, they open the royal blue door and there on the WELCOME mat the steaming pile of human excrement do you think they could tell it wasn't dog's? Bronwen was certain she and her friends hadn't meant it as an insult to the ruling class or anything, it was pure convenience, they bore no grudge, if anything they wanted to be *like* their daughters, she remembered watching them being walked home from school in their huge saddle shoes and fuzzy yellow angora sweaters with puffy sleeves and pleated Black Watch plaid skirts, they stood on their front stoops talking to the boys and Bronwen stared from across the street but they never noticed.

But all of this was happening when what really mattered was mapping out the smoothest roller skating route, seeing how much pure asphalt you could include, cobblestones were to be avoided at all costs and if you were lucky you had skates with those big lobster-like clamps that met over the middle of your shoe and never came off instead of those dinky ones that hooked like can openers to the soles of your shoes and ALWAYS came off, especially on sharp turns. And then there was the time when the great Doll Clothes War was raging and Bronwen nagged Katherine so much for a baby bunting set she had seen in Woolworth's that Katherine had thrown a coffee cup (empty) at her but had given her the money anyway in a fit of remorse. And later she got a stroller too but after she wheeled it outside realized it was meant for about a 4-year-old kid to push, while everyone else had these fantastic carriages with hoods and chrome-plated springs and plastic mattresses, huge things practically life-sized, but she kept pushing her little tin stroller along, getting a backache from bending so far down, her cheeks flaming but pretending nothing was amiss and anyway she felt sorry for them even if they did have pink satin quilts for their dolls because they went to parochial schools where you got number grades instead of letters and you might really get left back if you were dumb nobody in public school ever got left back. The Irish kids from the Catholic schools were wild demons as soon as the bell rang they tore out of their buildings, they terrified everyone they were all named Kevin they wore ties with stripes but used obscure dirty words like friggin' and threw watermelons off fruit stands in the summer and iceballs in the winter, Bronwen's friends always said it's because the nuns are so strict they use rulers on their bare hands.

Bronwen turned left onto West Fourth Street. She was ready to approach Washington Place and the building where she had lived with her father, off and on, after the divorce, at those times when her mother could no longer cope. Until he followed the sun all the way to Pasadena and everlasting ping-pong.

Past the family-style Italian restaurant with the blue and white menu permanently painted on the facade, boasting of 20 styles of calamari, the dry cleaners with the faded posters of women in ankle-length dresses smiling because they'd been "Martinized" (to this day Bronwen had no earthly idea what that was). Not too many changes.

The burning hot cement of the sidewalk finally began to make itself felt through the worn soles of her leather sandals (she really had to get new ones before the end of the summer) and an overwhelming craving for a ginger ale propelled Bronwen into the corner deli. Waiting to pay, she noticed something familiar about the man in front of her. There was a definite resemblance to Dirk Bogarde; a short, compact man with slightly protruding eyes and a full mouth... yes! It was her father's friend, what's-his-name the sculptor, who had that gigantic apartment on Christopher Street with all those statues on little pedestals, beige wall-to-wall carpets and the library with an actual ladder on wheels that he used to let her scoot around on. Should she tell him about Roger's death? She hadn't seen the guy for five or six years, it might not even be him ... While she hesitated, the man paid for his bottle of gin and disappeared. The moment was gone. Bronwen walked out onto the blazing pavement with her sweating bottle of ginger ale. She could almost smell the clay of ... Wolgang's, yes that was his name, Wolfgang's penthouse studio, that pleasing clay dust and clutter. He was a professional, unlike her father, who had only dabbled. She had always liked Wolfgang. Originally her father's instructor in some Adult Ed class, Wolfgang turned out to be a neighbor and the two men had become friends. She had felt a bond with Wolfgang, because somehow she and he knew that Roger was a pure amateur, that he'd be forever tinkering with the clay portrait bust of Bronwen that sat on an armature near her father's bed, draped with a damp cloth between sittings.

The apartment on Washington Place, only half a block away

now, had in fact been rented principally because of its large north-facing skylight. Perfect for her father's "sculpting," he told her excitedly as they climbed the three flights of stairs to the top, the morning he signed the lease. They had shared a large bag of freshly roasted cashew nuts as he paced about the small, bright rooms planning his new life.

At about the age of ten Bronwen had first started sitting for her father, at a rate of twenty-five cents an hour, but the head always resembled a wise 27-year-old no matter how many times her father started over between his frequent business trips. At first it was a joke between them, but they finally stopped talking about it and began to resign themselves to its changelessness. Once in a while Wolfgang would stop over for a drink and dispense a few crumbs of tactful advice. Bronwen didn't care as long as she kept getting paid.

Eventually, the head was replaced by a painfully accurate copy of The Discus Thrower, about twelve inches high. (Much use had been made of calipers.) One evening, when her father and Wolfgang were out having ground sirloin steaks at The Blue Mill Tavern, a bored Bronwen began to poke around for something to read. In the new Danish Modern bookcase, under some old copies of *LIFE* magazine, she stumbled on a cache of nudist magazines, filled with pictures of naked, flabby men and women surrounded by pine trees and holding volleyballs. The area between their legs was shadowy and indistinct, like Rembrandt portraits seen from too close up. This discovery shocked and shamed her and she never told anyone. She tried to rationalize it by telling herself her father needed accurate images for his sculpting projects.

Her greatest fantasy at that time was that Katherine would somehow marry Wolfgang, linking the two halves of her world together, but Bronwen knew this could never be. Even when he appeared at her eleventh birthday party, they kept their distance on opposite sides of the room.

Her best present that year was a Brownie Hawkeye camera, nestled in its cardboard nest next to the flash attachment that came with it. The next day her father took her to the opening of the huge black and white photography exhibit called *The Family of Man* at the Museum of Modern Art uptown. They drifted down the aisles past enormous montages of steelworkers and nursing Bedouin mothers, of Kansas farm families and Park Avenue debutantes. Afterwards, they went out for hot cocoa and donuts at the Mayflower Coffee Shop. What was that slogan? "As you go through life, Brother, let this always be your goal—keep your eye upon the donut, and not upon the hole." Something like that. It was a perfect day.

Felix was right about donuts. But now maybe he couldn't be her friend anymore. He had ruined everything.

Something bumped her from behind, and she whirled around, expecting to see Felix, ready to strike out at him, to shove him into the gutter. But it was only an old Italian woman in a black woolen headscarf, pushing a heavily laden two-wheeled shopping cart. The woman continued on her way, oblivious to their collision. She belonged here; Bronwen didn't. Not anymore.

Chapter 28

BACK in Cambridge, the summer resumed its jagged trajectory.

Often, Bronwen found herself squinting at Eric as he approached her from a distance, or hoping that when he came into a room he would be someone else.

She carried her yellowing copy of *The Notebooks of Malte Laurids Brigge* everywhere—on the train, to lunch. It gave her the perfect excuse not to talk to anyone about anything, and especially not about her father's death. She sat by herself in the cafeteria pretending to read it, stabbing with a fork at her cold french fries. If only Felix would plop down beside her and rattle on as if nothing had happened. He had managed to maintain a completely nocturnal schedule, so that their paths never crossed. Every morning a crisp, impersonal note awaited her, but she never saw him in the flesh. She knew he was also cranking out the final draft of his thesis, but anyway she missed him.

The one time she saw Caleb coming in through the main entrance she hastily returned her tray and escaped unseen through the kitchen. He had called her once but she had hung up the receiver at the sound of his voice. He didn't try again.

At her lab bench, she worked like a fiend, trying to keep her mind neutral and calm. She was a scientist, a scientist, a scientist. Wasn't she? If you said the word enough it sounded like a fringe cult. Scientist. Violinist. Rilke-ist. Daughter of suicide-ist. Her biology professor last year had told the class a story about an English scientist who had resumed writing in his lab notebook after World War II, simply using the next blank page without even remarking on the reason for the four-year lapse in entries. A dead father couldn't compare to that.

At the end of the second week after her return from New York, she was clinging tightly to Eric on the back of the BMW when she impulsively leaned forward and asked him if he had an inner life.

"What?" he shouted. "What the fuck do you mean by that?"

"Never mind!" she shouted back. "I have my answer!"

* * * *

The metal garter of her new white garter belt from the Woolworth's on 6th Ave was pressing into her right thigh something awful.

O Fath-er E-ter-nal .... How could her mother wear one of these every day? And Billy G. was poking her in the small of her back with his forefinger. At least he wasn't trying to snap her bra like he did during rehearsal.

She hated her dress, which had a design of fuzzy white flocked pear shapes sprinkled over stiff pink nylon, with a wide rose-colored sash. It seemed so babyish compared to Julie's princess style A-line white pique with the scoop neckline, that her stepmother had made from a Vogue pattern. It truly looked like a million dollars. Or at least thirty-five. Bronwen's looked fully the 6.95 (on sale) that her mother had paid at Orbach's. At least it was new.

BILLY STOP IT, I MEAN IT. THAT HURTS! He had managed to jab one of her breasts, underneath the purple graduation robe.

Mrs. Aronow was glaring at them. "That's right," she hissed as they passed. "Embarrass me in front of the entire ninth grade." Her mammoth bosom heaved under yards of navy blue gabardine. The white gardenia on her shoulder had a fine brown outline around every white petal. It spewed a heavy, almost tangible scent onto Bronwen as she walked past her favorite home room teacher, the one who had slipped her lunch money more than once when she had arrived without.

Mrs. A's wrathful gaze focused on Billy G., who seemed to literally grow smaller as their junior high class moved excruciatingly forward in lockstep to the recorded strains of "Pomp and Circumstance." Bronwen knew that her name was on the heavy ivory vellum of the programs, listed as "Valedictorian," and she knew that she had written a pretty damn good speech.

It was too bad her father couldn't have gotten the day off to hear her give it. He was somewhere in Pennsylvania, demonstrating toasters.

* * * *

Bronwen sat up. The dream again. The too-young dress, and then forgetting the last part of her speech.

She got up carefully so that Eric wouldn't wake, and went to the bathroom for a glass of water.

What, she wondered, had they played at her father's funeral? It should have been, by rights, "One Fine Day" from *Madama Butterfly*. But probably wasn't.

And it certainly wasn't "O Father Eternal." She turned off the light and walked back down the hallway. Maybe it should have been "O Father Sometimes."

It was the first Saturday that summer that she had stayed home and slept in. Eric was already up and out. Bronwen, in khaki bermudas and the genuine striped fisherman's jersey, was on her second sesame bagel when the doorbell rang.

The mailman handed her a large square white envelope with no return address and what seemed to be a shoebox, wrapped in heavy brown paper and lacquered with many yards of Scotch tape. Through the tape she could recognize her Aunt Lucy's delicate old-lady penmanship. The box was postmarked Pasadena.

First the envelope. Inside was a piece of white cardboard with a small round mirror glued to it. Underneath, in large handprinted red letters, it said

WANTED! YOU! - AT FELIX'S DOCTORAL CELEBRATION BASH!

Date: Aug. 20, 1963 -   Dress: Of course
Place: The Kilmer's - Bring: Your favorite   booze

Felix had pencilled a note:

Be there or be square, Bron-one. Bring Eric if you must.

All's fair that ends well .... and it did end fairly well, didn't it? Fare thee well—but come.

Felix

So he had finally done it. Paulette must be euphoric.

Bronwen found herself rereading his note, admiring his large, wild handwriting. There was not much left of the summer. She would be leaving a few days after the party.

A sudden dampness between her legs made her rush to the bathroom to check for the long-awaited dark red dot that would signal freedom, happiness, joy unending.

But no. She was apparently not getting her period. She was now a full three weeks late. No matter how she scrutinized the white cotton crotch, there was not the slightest evidence of blood. The bright Saturday morning was blackening at the edges like burning newsprint.

Back in the kitchen, the homely brown package was waiting on the table for her. She might as well get it over with.

Inside the shoebox she found the following, in no particular order:

canceled cheques for her orthodonture with Dr. Vernon Swann, of Pasadena fame, totaling 3,700 dollars—almost three year's worth of college tuition;

a new passport, unused, bearing a photo identical to the one she had received in the mail a few weeks ago;

an Honorable Discharge from the Navy in 1946;

a rolled up Bachelor's Diploma in Engineering from Purdue University, class of 1932;

a photo of her father and an unknown woman in a strapless black cocktail dress, in a cardboard frame with the logo of The Stork Club in Manhattan;

and, held securely together with a thick red rubber band that was beginning to dry out and crack along one edge, every letter she had ever written to him.

She put the box down on the rug at her feet, unable to open the package of letters, mostly written on crinkly pink Crane's stationery. After so many dry days, the tears were finally here.

Chapter 29

LEMON juice on sliced bananas. Her father's favorite breakfast.

"It's our secret," he'd say. "Isn't it weird how perfectly the sensations complement each other?" Smooth and sharp. Sweet and sour. Like her father's moods. Before Four Roses—and after.

He taught her to crave guava shells paired with slices of Philadelphia cream cheese, floating in thick amber syrup. The circles of grainy, firm fruit; the neat rectangles of soft, cool cheese. Maybe during that year in Brazil, engineering graduate in exile, he'd acquired these exotic tastes. Along with the unwearable pair of handsewn shoes, automatically made one size too small by the cobbler used to the vanity of his countrymen.

"Say something in Portuguese, please, Dad," and he would, the soft words lingering in the air over their breakfast table on the weekends when she was allowed to stay overnight. He was not like anyone else's father, not by far.

Bronwen finished weighing the last batch of substrate needed for the enzyme reaction. She was almost ready to start the five-hour experiment that was going to conclusively confirm her discovery of the summer. She knew people thought it was weird that she had gone back to work so soon after her father's death, but there was simply no money for flying to a funeral in California. And anyway, trained engineer that her father was, he'd have wanted her to be doing exactly what she was doing. Wouldn't he? The alternate possibility was that he had tried to sabotage her. That he had deliberately punished her for daring to have a mind and body of her own.

Pushing the idea aside, she kept busy, lined up the clean pipettes next to the spectrophotometer and went to look for another stopwatch. That line of thought was not helpful. Once she'd started the reaction, she'd take a reading every fifteen seconds. The brighter the yellow of the dye, the more enzyme product being released. Leave it to an Italian to come up with such an aesthetic procedure. Bronwen smiled, thinking of the first time she'd encountered Professor

Baldessori. After that fateful lecture, her whole life had changed.

Her heart was doing its flippy pre-experiment dance. Although the evening was no longer young, she felt rested and calm. Ready to rock and roll. When the door behind her creaked open, she spun around. The clock above the open door showed it to be 9:48. It was Felix. His timing couldn't have been worse.

"Am I interrupting anything important?" This was said in a wistful tone she had never heard before. And what a question, coming from Felix!

He stood in the doorway, tipping himself in and out of the room. She had never seen him so subdued.

"To be honest, yes. I was just about to begin that long series, a repeat of what I was doing last week. I left you a note yesterday." He was making her nervous. "I've got to start in a few minutes."

"Maybe I could help you?"

"Not this time. I'm all psyched up to do it myself. Really. But thanks for the offer." She glanced up at the clock.

"I need to talk to you now. I can wait in my car until you're done. Give you a ride home."

"Well ....I was planning to sleep on the cot." Damn. That was a mistake. Now he'd know where she was all night.

"No, I really need to talk to you tonight. When you're finished. Just hang your lab coat out the window as a signal and I'll come up."

She couldn't think. The ice in the bucket was melting.

"Okay. Coat out the window, we'll talk a few minutes, then you'll go. But there's really nothing to say. I don't need to ever talk or think about what happened."

"No. There's something I have to tell you. About Paulette and myself. Everything is different." And he was gone.

Bronwen turned back to her test tubes. So the rumor about Paulette's pregnancy was true. But she didn't want to know anything about it. The less she knew about Felix's private life the happier she'd be.

"My, aren't we the industrious little Madame Curie?"

"AAAh! Dammit, you scared me, Caleb, I almost knocked my set-up over!"

"But you didn't, did you?"

The evening was getting out of control. Caleb, in his Converse high-tops, had crept up behind her and placed his large, warm hands over her eyes. She recognized him instantly by the odor of wine, cigarette smoke and a sweet, musty smell like the far corner of a secondhand bookstore. Underneath ran the sharp lavender scent of Yardley's shaving soap. She wondered wildly if Caleb used the kind that came in wooden bowls, so often her last-minute choice for Father's Day. One or two half-used containers always lurked, gathering dust, in the medicine cabinet of any apartment her dad occupied.

Caleb remained at her elbow. The ice in her bucket was melting. "You have to leave *NOW*. I'll never get this finished. I mean it."

He moved off to one side. "Mind if I watch? Science-wise, I'm really more of a voyeur. And I'm definitely a connoisseur of good technique. Did you know that?"

"No, and no ... And I don't have time to kid around. You really have to go."

"You're not avoiding me? Dinner tomorrow? My bed ... er ...place?"

She glanced at him, prepared to make a remark that would wipe the smirk right off his face. But his eyes held hers, and she couldn't remember the last time Eric had actually looked at her.

"Okay ... but you really have to go *NOW*."

Finally, alone, she turned up the radio and began. But there was no way that she'd let herself get enmeshed with Caleb again. She'd call him in the morning to cancel.

Down in the parking lot, Caleb passed Felix's VW and heard the loud snores emanating from within. He surmised domestic problems and opted not to stick a pencil in Felix's open mouth.

Indeed, Caleb was feeling too good to do even a modicum of mischief to his fellow man.

Chapter 30

FELIX was pumping Eric's bowing hand vigorously, squeezing the fingers hard. Bronwen could see Eric wincing and trying to pull his hands out of Felix's grasp.

"... heard so much about you, a revelation, really, to finally, um ... to ..." With his free left hand, Felix plucked at the crotch of his unaccustomedly tight khaki pants.

"Yeah, me too," Eric mumbled, beginning to show real concern that he might never wield a violin bow again. He gave a last valiant tug and his fingers broke loose in a wide arc, swinging due west and neatly clipping the passing Dr. Bergenstrasser in the small of her back.

"Mein Gott!" She spit out her chicken liver, water chestnut and bacon appetizer, which flew through the air and landed with a messy splash in Paulette's almost-full glass of lukewarm Liebfraumilch.

Bronwen, horrified, had seen it all. Paulette looked up in confusion from her conversation with their host, Department Chairman Dr. Kilger (a.k.a. Dr. Killjoy, or The Big K). She and Paulette locked gazes for a bare instant, and from the expression in Paulette's big brown eyes Bronwen realized that Paulette knew nothing. And really, there was nothing to know. The incident in New York was just a fit brought on by impending fatherhood and the pressures of the academic snakepit, best forgotten. Feeling Bronwen's steady gaze, Paulette pointed a finger at the mess in her glass and smiled a sheepish smile. Bronwen could see that for the first time in her life, Paulette felt and was beautiful, truly beatific in her green striped Marimekko sundress with just a slight swelling at the belly where none had ever been. She must be at least three months pregnant by now. Well, at least Felix had finished his damn thesis. Paulette had stuck it out this far. She and Felix would probably make it. Bronwen hoped Felix wouldn't be stupid enough to *confess*.

In the background, Bronwen could hear Eric apologizing profusely to Dr. Bergenstrasser. He had just recognized her as the star of a recent rally on behalf of the newly created women scientist's subgroup of The Concerned Scientists Union. A splinter group had formed an unofficial sub-subgroup called Scientists Against the Coming War in S.E. Asia, known as SAW-SEA, or SAUCY for short. It was widely speculated that Dr. B.'s anti- war position might have been the final straw in The Big K's decision not to grant her tenure. They needed all the government grants they could get in the coming year, what with the defense budget beginning to chip away at the old Sputnik-inspired glut of research grants, and she was becoming too outspoken, writing to the *New York Times* about analogies to the Nuremburg Trials and things like that. Her claims that she couldn't repeat Dr. K's lab results could always be suppressed somehow, but the political stuff was too public. Bronwen knew that she had even testified at a special Congressional hearing just last week.

Felix had done everything he could to keep her on, risking his own tenuous position in the process. He had even offered her a job as his lab technician—she, who had twenty years more experience than he and at least as good a brain! Felix saw his attempts as a kind of Diary of Anne Frank scenario in reverse, his lab the attic and himself the solid citizen. Of course, just in case, he kept his Canadian citizenship alive and well so any child of his could always have a legal escape route.

But Inge had decided to retire early and go live with her mother in the countryside outside of Basel. She just didn't have any fight left in her. Bronwen had heard there was a variety of rare Spotted Black Rose or something that Inge said she wanted to cultivate in her mother's already locally renowned garden. In the meantime, she was becoming quite alarmingly sloshed.

All this flitted through Bronwen's brain in the horrible seconds that the "Angels on Horseback" appetizer (or whatever the Hell they were called) was flying through the air. She jumped when Eric put his sweaty palm on the back of her neck.

"Listen. I don't think I can hang out here any longer. I promised I'd come. I came. Now can I go?"

"Of course. Far be it from me to pressure you into being a civilized human being for two hours."

"Ha, ha, so funny I forgot to laugh. Can you get a ride back with Felix or someone? How long is this wild orgy going to last?"

"Yes-I-can-get-a-ride-back-with-Felix-or-someone. See you later."

Bronwen turned her back and stomped around the edges of a large pink rhododendron bush, almost tripping over a long black-clad leg, the knee patched with fragments of red bandanna. The owner of the leg was softly reciting "The Rime of The Ancient Mariner" to his kneecap.

Caleb. Damn.

"Ho ho. The young Bronwen. Women, women, everywhere, and not a drop to drink." He raised the empty bottle in salute to her.

"The *Very Ancient* Caleb. And apparently you've had quite enough already."

"By whose standards? Always the judgments. Don't you ever get tired of being on your high horse? Especially when you and I know that behind that mild-mannered exterior, it's really Lady Godiva that..."

"Shut up!"

Caleb stiffened.

"You swore you'd never bring that up again. I wasn't in my right mind. We were both drunk. Can't we just agree to forget about it?"

He stood up, brushing freshly cut grass from his pantslegs.

"Fine. Done. I can be a gentleman of the old school, when required. But even courtly lovers have their price."

Before she knew what was happening, Caleb bent over and pressed his soft mouth lightly onto hers. Again she marveled that such a hard, bony person could have lips so full and warm. He smelled and tasted of the rosé wine he'd been drinking but she didn't mind. The vodka and tonic began to sing along her nerves.

"Now. Go back to the party. Enjoy. Shan't discuss this again. See you around. Look forward to discussing enzyme kinetics with you. Someday. Ta ta." Caleb turned and in three long steps he was gone.

Unsteadied by alcohol and Caleb's kiss, Bronwen retraced her path around the rhododendron bush. Her least favorite flowers, they seemed to grow like weeds in Portland. It reminded her that she'd be back on campus in less than two weeks.

In the distance, people were beginning to gather around the huge square cake Paulette had baked for the party. Bronwen tried to walk briskly, but the narrow heels of her dress-up pumps (almost unworn since high school graduation) kept sinking into the moist topsoil of the lawn. A clot of nausea in her stomach was starting to spread. It couldn't be Caleb's baby. It couldn't. But, of course, it could.

As she approached the crowd, she heard the tall visiting English geneticist say, "Who's the girl?" and someone else reply, "Oh, just Eric Breuner's girlfriend."

Just Eric Breuner's *girl*friend? Her eyes smarting, she made a quick detour to the right, and found herself behind a large lilac bush. Every breath she took hurt. She counted to ten. Eric Breuner's girlfriend?

She kept walking (just Eric Breuner's *pregnant* girlfriend), piercing the soil deeply with every step, past the table with the blue gingham tablecloth and the mammoth slab of chocolate cake. Earlier she had peeked at it. On the bittersweet chocolate icing (Felix's favorite) Paulette had traced in white buttercream frosting an outline of a smirking B.subtilis bacterium shaking hands with a potbellied stick figure of Felix in a graduate's mortarboard. "CONGRATULATIONS, DR. FELIX!" it said. "You did it! We love you!"

Bronwen continued down the side path and was finally standing under the towering maple at the edge of the front yard. Dr. Kilger's house was on one of the nicest streets in Cambridge, and it wouldn't take her more than half an hour to walk home. She didn't need a ride. The air would do her good.

She leaned over to remove the impractical shoes and set off. Eric Breuner's pregnant, *barefoot* goddamned girlfriend. But not for long. You could bet on that. If she'd had any doubts before, they were gone now. Her mother had already made *that* mistake for both of them.

The uneven bricks of the sidewalk were pleasantly warm against the soles of her feet. She wished she had managed to scarf up a piece of Paulette's cake to eat as she walked. She also hoped the English geneticist would get food poisoning and die. Oh, well, she could dream, couldn't she? She'd always been good at that.

Chapter 31

"HERE." Felix thrust an 8 by 11 yellow manila envelope at Bronwen. "Read it when you get on the plane." They were standing at the United Airlines check-in counter, waiting while the ticket agent slipped a tag on Bronwen's olive canvas duffel bag with the mysterious black stenciled numbers, probably from the Korean War. Felix and Bronwen stared at the bag as if they expected a dancing girl to pop out and dispel the tension that hummed between them. Since that night when he'd come and told her about Paulette's pregnancy and begged her to obliterate the scene in New York from her memory they had hardly talked.

"If you need any ... recommendations...for graduate school," Felix began, tapping his empty pipe on the counter, pointedly avoiding her eyes. "Just ask. Be glad to." He loosened his underwear with his free hand and began to hum softly.

"I will. I definitely will. You've been so ..."

"Right. Listen, I've got to get back. Paulette isn't feeling too well and she asked me to transfer some cultures for her."

He looked at Bronwen with such a direct gaze that she felt the outline of her whole body sizzling in the air. With his forefinger he touched her bare shoulder, bony and brown under the blue and white striped tank top.

"This is it," he said. "This is really it."

No words, none at all, formed themselves in Bronwen's mind.

She willed time to pass, and she let herself go blank. When she snapped out of her trance, the United agent was handing back her ticket and asking if she wanted a window seat. She was alone, ready for whatever was coming.

She decided to stock up on gum and maybe treat herself to a copy of *The New Yorker*, now that she was blessedly far from the scrutiny of Eric and his buddies. As she switched the manila envelope to her less sweaty hand and hoisted her bulging carry-on bag onto her back, she caught sight of Caleb pushing his way through the crowd, head and skinny shoulders above everyone else. Her first thought was that he was going to try to stop her from having the abortion. Before she could flee, he was upon her, dark glasses, torn jeans and all.

He was terribly nervous and kept looking back over his shoulder.

"How come Eric isn't here? Are you sure he's not around somewhere?"

Bronwen glared at him. She was fighting nausea.

"Not that it's any of your business, but today is the first day of the freshman Genetics Survey seminar that he's teaching. He couldn't possibly miss the first session."

Caleb continued to stare at her. Something in her began to collapse. "Well, actually, he hates airports and he probably wouldn't have come anyway, he gets nervous when I fly, the smell of airplane fuel makes him sick ..."

Caleb inhaled sharply. "Excuse me, Bronwen, I may be speaking out of turn here, but that's all a crock and you know it." He paused to catch his breath. "He's an overbearing little shit and aside from the fact that he knows how to promote himself and his admittedly better-than-average brain, THERE'S NOTHING THERE! There's nothing about him that fits you. Even remotely. He sleeps around—no, wait, let me finish—when you're not here, and brags about your ass when you are. He doesn't love you. He doesn't need you and I do. It sounds like more bullshit but it's true."

They stood there by the candy counter, while impatient travelers reached around them for Chiclets and Lifesavers.

Bronwen stood unmoving, aware only that her face radiated heat while the blood in her veins was rapidly chilling.

"You don't know ..." she began.

"I do!" Caleb was shouting. "I do know. You know it too .... I don't have to prove anything to you. And I am NOT a goddamned theory!" People were beginning to stare. "And your life is not some geneticist's wet dream of an EXPERIMENT. You can't just do it over and over until you get it right!"

His face was very pale except for two bright red splotches on his cheekbones, blooming in a meadow of freckles. It took all her willpower not to reach up and touch his face.

He wasn't finished. "For Christ's sake, take a chance once in a while, follow your instincts—if you haven't fucking AUTOCLAVED them to death!" A fit of coughing finally silenced him.

"You're not being fair." She fought for control, for the shock of his words to wear off. She needed the familiar surge of anger that would help her get out of this mess. "And, anyway, my instincts tell me you're crazy."

"Maybe. But that's a really cheap shot. You know I'm the only human being in years who's had the nerve to tell you something you might not like hearing. And that's because—

ha ha—the classic cliché—I'm a loser with nothing to lose! I know you don't love ME. You're in love with your future.... Besides, dear child, I'm dropping out. Not going to continue wasting anyone's time. Including my own. I've already said good-bye to Felix. He's one doofus I'm going to miss. I'm leaving for Alabama next week. I think I can be more useful there—or at least less useless. See you in my next incarnation."

"LAST CALL FOR FLIGHT 124 to Portland! Now boarding at Gate 12!"

They looked at each other. "I'm not flattered that you *need* me," Bronwen began, "I don't want anybody to need me, don't you get it ...."

Caleb put his hand on her lips. "Fine, fine, fine. I get it, a little late maybe, but what the Hell. The woman is an island unto herself. Fine. I get it, I got it, good-bye."

She saw the back of his head zig-zagging through the crowd, and the summer was over. Gathering her various satchels and the shockingly heavy green canvas bookbag, she turned towards the departure gate. The lip Caleb had touched felt strangely warm and swollen.

At least on the plane she would be safe from these sudden encounters, these accusations. It was too much. And

Barbara Riddle

somehow, none of it seemed to have anything to do with her, not really.

Relief and nausea competed for dominance as she slip-slopped up the entrance ramp and down into the belly of the jet.

"Could I have a Canada Dry ginger ale?" Waiting while the stewardess rummaged around to find this irritatingly specific choice, Bronwen let herself fully acknowledge the meaning of this persistent early morning nausea: there could be no doubt. Swollen breasts, four weeks overdue—she had to be pregnant. In her wallet was $250 in cash, Eric's share of the abortion fee if a doctor's examination in Portland confirmed the already obvious. He had called a friend who knew someone who knew of a clinic in Seattle; safe, no questions asked. Her classes started in a week.

"Ice?" The impeccably groomed young woman was handing a tumbler to Bronwen. Her ponytail jounced as she turned her head from side-to-side. They were almost the same age. Bronwen felt 100 years older.

"Thank you."

"Are you alright? Can I bring you a pillow or a blanket?" It was ten o'clock in the morning and she was already being treated like an invalid. Interesting word, that—not valid. In valid. That was exactly how she felt. She hadn't told Eric that the baby might not be his. Hadn't she been faithful for three years?

The stewardess was still waiting.

"I'm fine, thanks. Just nervous. I'm fine."

Jaunty pony-tail moved on.

Next to Bronwen, a red-faced man in a tan cowboy hat (the ghost of Uncle Homer?) demanded to know why they hadn't left the airport yet. Bronwen hadn't noticed, and now didn't care when she realized they were still taxi-ing around in circles. She was in no hurry to land back at her other life.

She managed a weak smile in the direction of this only too fleshy apparition, and shrugged her ignorance of all things aeronautic. He went back to his crisp *Time* magazine, dated July 26, 1963 (only a month old!), the blandly distractive power of which she desperately coveted. If she could just get through the next 6 hours without throwing up on old Tex and his lavishly turquoise-studded silver belt buckle.

He seemed to be annoyed at what he was reading and she peeked over his broad cowboy-shirted shoulder. There was a two-page spread on recent civil rights demonstrations in the South, and a picture entitled "Atlanta's Integrated Pool," with three dark-skinned teenagers, followed by a white one, walking down a ramp of wooden steps into a public swimming pool. The blurry photo was subtitled "For others the water was rougher," and further down the page was a city-by-city summary of incidents.

One paragraph caught her attention:

"Tuscaloosa, Alabama. The University of Alabama Board of Trustees filed notice that it would ask the Circuit Court of Appeals for permission to oust newly admitted Negro students Vivian Malone and James Hood. In Atlanta, a 15-year-old Negro boy taking part in a restaurant sit-in was stabbed by a white customer ...."

Her seatmate flipped the magazine closed and tossed it in his elaborately-tooled leather briefcase. He closed his eyes.

Alabama. Caleb had said he was going to Alabama. Of course.

Cowboy hat tipped over his eyes, ol' Tex was snoring now, his fastened seatbelt awkwardly riding piggyback on top of his massive silver belt buckle. She longed to get her hands on that magazine. She would have to wait.

Alabama. Sun so hot I froze to death, Susanna don't you cry. Oh Susanna. Rained so hard the day I left. Don't you dare cry for me. Alabama. The maybe father of the baby she wasn't going to have wasn't such a loser after all. If only he didn't go and get himself killed. Even if she never saw him again, she wanted to think of him as alive, alive and warm.

Suddenly exhausted, Bronwen tried to settle into a position that guaranteed the least bodily contact with Tex. He was snoring so loudly she doubted if she could sleep, tired as she was. Then she noticed that the manila envelope Felix had shoved in her hand was now lying on the floor along with her precious *New Yorker*. She supposed it was some final paperwork the University needed her to fill out so she could get credit for the summer. Might as well do it now so she could mail it when she arrived in Portland. The plane picked up speed and began its final fling down the exit runway as she opened the envelope and pulled out the manuscript inside. At the top of the page she was listed as a co-author on her first scientific paper, along with Felix and the toothsome Italian.

Chapter 32

"SO, Mrs., ah ... Green," the young doctor said, glancing down at his notes.

"Congratulations. You are approximately seven and a half weeks pregnant. You can get dressed now. Come to my front office when you're ready." He was scribbling on a prescription pad. Like Eric, he was left-handed.

"I've written you a prescription for vitamins. And you've got to start taking extra calcium right away."

She had picked his name from the phone book by closing her eyes and putting her finger down on the page. He was young and clean-cut, and had a small office in an anonymous 1940's office building in downtown Portland. And she had actually purchased a wedding ring for 99¢ at Woolworth's. My God. Her first conception.

"Here you go. Vitamins, and a date for our next check-up. I'll be glad to take you on, unless you had other ... unless you have a family doctor or someone? Will you be delivering in Portland?"

She had to get out of this room. "I'm not sure. Thank you. I'll call you. I'd like to pay today for this visit." She handed him two tens and a five and stumbled out the door.

On the street, she walked blindly forward, crossing whenever she came to a green light. The phrase "first conception" kept coming into her head. Calcium. Something inside her craved calcium .... She imagined herself dropping out, moving to Montana, raising a genius child and spinning wool from her flock of imported sheep ...

If she loved Eric, wouldn't this ... this creation be worth keeping? For the first time, she realized that she didn't know whether she loved Eric. And even if she did, she certainly had no idea how to take care of a baby. A mother, her? She didn't even know how to be a daughter. She couldn't even keep her father alive.

"Miss, you'd better watch yourself." She was about to step off the curb into the path of a city bus. An obese woman with a head of cheerful gray curls and huge flat feet in blue tennis shoes had grabbed her elbow. Subdued, Bronwen followed her onto the bus, which was headed towards the campus. Her rescuer came to sit next to her, getting up from her original seat.

"One of these beatniks, eh? From the college? My grandson was up at the school there, he had the time of his life. Of course he lives in Virginia now, I only see him over the holidays, he's something in the Government, would you believe I'm a great-grandmother?"

The leaves were beginning to change color, and the afternoon light had a new chill to it. It was three days after Labor Day. She had better make reservations for the flight to Seattle immediately.

They were so young. She had not expected them to be so young. They sat, eyes staring straight ahead or at their shoes, waiting. Several were with women obviously their mothers—permanent-waved and tight-lipped, clutching purses in various shapes and shades of plastic on their laps. Bronwen was the only one in the room not wearing a skirt.

The brown and orange plaid linoleum floor was faded but passably clean. A sweetish chemical smell reminded her of frog-dissection day in the 7th grade, and she stifled an impulse to call out loudly that it was time for everyone to line up for their trays and their frogs .... Oh, Mr. Cohen. Come and get us, let's do this one over.

The "clinic" door with its unmarked pane of frosted glass banged shut behind her. This was the most dangerous thing she had ever done. She stood there, trying to get her bearings. To the left was the crowded waiting room, where a few pairs of eyes darted in her direction and then back to their inward gazing. To her right was a large oak desk where a white-capped nurse (one hoped) sat sentry. She was flipping through a thick green appointment book and saying goodbye to someone while she erased an entry. When she put down the receiver and looked inquiringly in her direction, Bronwen inadvertently took a step backwards. Then, reeled in by the nurse's eyes, she walked directly to the Reception Desk, her new hand-made Cambridge sandals squeaking loudly. Her name and appointment were quickly verified. Then came The Question.

"How many weeks?"

"How many ... oh. Not quite eight weeks." Bronwen's voice boomed out along the corridors of what she now could see was a fairly extensive suite of rooms, all with closed doors and unmarked panes of frosted glass.

"Eight weeks?" The yellow pencil stopped moving and White Cap looked up. Her voice was almost imperceptibly sharper, but hushed, commanding Bronwen to answer at a similar volume. "You'll have to be treated this afternoon. The doctor can see you back here for a full procedure in two hours. Don't eat lunch. Do you have the fee? In cash?"

Bronwen nodded dumbly, uncertain whether to rummage in her bag for the envelope containing the five hundred dollars.

"Good. Bring it with you. You'll give it to me before we begin." Then she allowed herself a thin little smile. "And don't be nervous. He's very good." The phone rang and she picked it up, dismissing Bronwen from her consciousness.

Two hours to kill in Seattle, no food allowed. Space Needle, here I come.

* * * *

"You're late!" White Cap hissed, as all heads turned to watch Bronwen's clumsy entrance. "Follow me!"

Clad only in the archetypal hospital smock, Bronwen was lying flat on her back behind one of those frosted glass doors that you always saw in German detective movies, right before the cameras pan in on the corpse. Her feet were gently being positioned in cold metal footrests by an older and more motherly White Cap. When Bronwen realized that her ankles were being strapped to the stirrups, she raised her head in protest. "We need to ... so you won't ... kick the doctor when he ... we can't use any anesthetic, you see."

Indeed, Bronwen was beginning to see very well.

"Now, young lady, we can't have this, can we?"

Bronwen shook her head no. No, we can't have this.

"A little pinch, that's a good girl. Alright nurse, let's begin ... Now, young lady, this is not going to be any picnic, but you're going to be brave and we're going to send you out of here and back to school and you're going to be just fine. You can hold onto the nurse's arm if you need to. Here we go."

A razor blade the size of a paint scraper was loose inside her uterus, dragged by a metallic rat with fangs like a rattlesnake. A psychotic Gene Kelly was tap-dancing in football cleats on the walls of her womb. "Ohhhhhhh! Ohhhhhhmy god!" She looked down and saw that she was digging her nails into the freckled forearm of the maternal White Cap—were the screams Bronwen's or the nurse's? She didn't know, didn't care, was just hanging on for the ride. Caleb's face floated in and out of her consciousness, he was biting her shoulder and she was moaning and kissing him, pressing her mouth hard against his cheekbone.

"We're almost there, young lady, now that wasn't so bad, was it, just a little bit more, we have to do this right, there. Alright. Take a deep breath, exhale, deep breath, let it out. Now you go back to that school, and you finish up, and we don't want to see you back here, you hear me? You take good care of yourself." And he was gone. She never really did see his face. She would never have been able to identify him in a police line-up.

It was over. She could feel warm blood trickling slowly out, but there was no pain. And no baby. She was just plain Bronwen again.

"Here are some extra pads, and there's a room over here for you to rest in. The doctor wants you to lie down for an hour at least before you go out."

The nurse guided her into a small room with no windows. A clean white sheet was tucked around a brown vinyl examining couch, and a faded pink cotton thermal blanket was folded neatly at the bottom. "Try and nap a little if you can."

Bronwen lay down and pulled the blanket over her. Caleb must be somewhere in Cambridge, packing his books and listening to his Bob Dylan albums. She closed her eyes. And Felix ... was probably just getting up. Looking for a clean shirt. She sat up. She loved him. Jesus H. Christ. She loved Felix!

The operator was asking her to hold on. Her party was going to accept the collect call. Bronwen jiggled her knee, trying to keep her leg from cramping up. She was in a phone booth at the Seattle airport, with twenty minutes to go before her flight left for Portland. She had promised to call Eric after it was all over.

"Hi! Yeah, I'm o.k., really. But it was bad. Really bad. No, the doctor was fine, it was clean and everything. But it hurt. A lot. No, they couldn't use any, because I had already eaten and they were afraid I would throw up and choke....So they didn't use any anes ... What? I can't hear you. Oh ... great! That's the Fellowship you wanted ... yeah, I know. That's really fantastic ... Eric? I won't ever do this again. It was the right thing for now, but someday I might want ... We might want ... and it feels like there could be damage, you know, if this happened again." A young sailor in dress whites stopped near her booth, puffing on a cigarette. He looked her up and down and moved on.

"I'm not blaming you for anything. ...Listen, I know that. It just happened. I want you to know that I won't do it again, that's all. How do you mean I sound different? Well I *am* different. Anyway I have to go. Write to me?" She hung up, and continued to stand in the booth, staring at the instructions for long-distance dialing.

She couldn't love Felix. It must be gratitude, or even pity, that she felt. She loved *Eric*. Of course she did. Everyone knew that. And Caleb wasn't even on planet Earth.

On her way to the Boarding Gate, she bought a postcard

of the infamous Space Needle—official reason for her "holiday excursion"—to send to her mother.

"Old Seattle saying," Bronwen wrote, "You never enter the same airport twice."

When she was finally settled in her window seat with an itchy blue wool blanket tucked around her shoulders, she realized she was completely exhausted. Letting her mind go blank, watching the billowing clouds rush by, Bronwen waited to feel sad but felt only relief and a slight throbbing in her pelvis. Her life had been given back to her. *What was she going to do with it?*

She closed her eyes and saw the abortionist's busy face, framed by her raised knees. He could have made her feel like a criminal, a sordid sexpot. Instead, he had dispensed solace and advice like the kindliest of grandfathers. It seemed, somehow, that he cared more about her future than Eric did. Maybe in Eric's mind they didn't *have* a future.

Vague memories of the doctor's Black Watch plaid bowtie came into focus. He and she would be linked forever, like skydivers holding hands and grinning as they jumped from the belly of the plane.

A bell dinged annoyingly overhead and the sudden jerk of her seat warned that they were beginning their descent. She opened her eyes and realized it was still the same day. Back to ground zero in thirteen hours.

Chapter 33

IT WAS weird, truly incomprehensible. Baffling. How had it happened? From a young girl's obsession with what made warm furry puppies tick to this—alone in a stockroom filled with broken distillation equipment. Bronwen fought tears.

Her mood didn't improve when she sought refuge in the normally comforting intimacy of the cramped Chemistry Department library. It was four-thirty in the afternoon on the third day after her abortion. She sat on the floor and stared up at the huge maroon volumes of Chemical Abstracts. All those authors whose papers would never be read again. All that buried life's blood. The futile quest for immortality.

She stood, wiped her nose on the sleeve of her sweatshirt and picked up a copy of *Nature*, whose quaint Britishisms usually distracted her from incipient depressions. The thin journal opened easily to the Obituary page. "Professor

Lambeth-Cruickshank will be long remembered for his stimulating rock and fossil hunts, which inspired two generations of students to ..." Good grief! Was everybody dead or dying? If she stayed in this room for another minute she'd disappear from the face of the earth.

Throwing the journal down on the library table, she admitted defeat. She had to get out of this room. The dining hall would be just opening up. She'd come back later and check on her lab project.

Bronwen pushed open the swinging door. This year was clearly not going to be like the last, when she had joked her way through the most boring courses and posted a sign proclaiming Emerson's "Consistency is the Hobgoblin of Small Minds" over her Quantitative Analysis bench. Only the instructor was unamused. And, needless, to say, her grade had reflected that. This time she couldn't screw around. Not if she wanted to build on the lucky break that Felix had provided her over the summer. He was expecting big things from her. Everyone was.

Just before she reached the end of the hall, the huge framed Periodic Chart of the Elements caught her attention. Bronwen hadn't really looked at it for years. She scrutinized the mysterious alchemical abbreviations: Au for gold, Ag for silver. And there was her favorite: Argon. The inert gas. That was how she felt: BRon— an obscure inert mineral with no special commercial use or aesthetic value.

Suddenly she wheeled around and headed straight back to the library. Still wearing her jacket, she sat down, grabbed a yellow legal pad and pencil from somebody's clutter and began to release the words that had been forming since her plane had lifted off the tarmac in Boston ten days ago:

"Dear Felix," she scribbled ... and then paused. For a minute she sat as if in a trance, then resumed.

"All of a sudden I don't know what I wanted to tell you. It was so clear and now I've gone blank. I am so scared of saying the wrong things. Again. Forgive me if I am not clear. What I want to write about is love (small l). This past summer, watching you in the lab, I saw a man in love with his mind and with using his mind to unravel the twists and turns of the world. You didn't care how you appeared to me or to anyone else. I had never met anyone like you. You also didn't seem to care how I appeared, either. You only noticed me if I said smart or funny things. I loved that about you. And you made me feel like I was part of a very special group. It wasn't just you and me.

That all changed later, after my father's death. I don't know what I said or did but somehow you started treating me like a woman. I hated that. But I never hated you. You have to know that. It's just that you weren't in that sphere for me—

and anyway, you were someone else's mate, someone I liked, and it never even occurred to me that what happened could possibly happen. Am I stupid or just naïve? Or maybe you think I was opportunistic? I honestly don't think so. I wanted you to love my mind as much as I loved yours and I really wanted to make you laugh. Eric never laughed at my jokes— not with his whole body, the way you did.

I will never forget you, Felix. And when I say never, I mean it.

Your aspiring acolyte, Bronwen

P.S. At the risk of being misinterpreted—I miss you.

P.P.S. Organic chemistry is insanely logical! Hooray!! Am going back to the lab after dinner—wish you were there to greet me with a maple cruller or two ...." She folded this letter neatly and put it in her jacket pocket.

The doors of the Life Sciences West building clanged behind her like prison gates in a Hollywood B-movie. Loneliness constricted her throat. Zipping up her Army surplus parka, she bent her head into the late afternoon breeze. In the pouch-like pocket of her jacket, next to the letter, she felt for the presence of her trusty ubiquitous Rilke volume, her shield against unwanted dinner conversation. What she wouldn't give for the sight of an unshaven, rumpled Felix emerging from his trusty VW.

At least the challenge of Krumley's infamously difficult Organic Chemistry lab course would keep her from having too much spare brooding time. She would be handed a motley mixture of noxious chemicals each month, composition known only to the elfin Dr. Krumley. Her task was to separate, purify and identify the components as quickly and elegantly as possible—unsurpassable training for the time in the not-too-distant future when they would be on their own with no kindly professors to guide their research efforts.

Today she had sat through Krumley's introductory lecture, still bleeding but in no physical pain other than occasional uterine contractions. Just another co-ed there to soak up his words of wisdom. He smiled impishly as he handed over her very own Mystery Mix, and wished her luck.

Although it seemed impossible that *anything* could be extracted from what looked like a paste of tar and oatmeal coated with salad oil, she had dutifully followed the specified ritual; heat, distill, rinse the residue with universal solvent. She left a flask of warm liquid smelling like cleaning fluid, neatly covered with foil, on the lab bench to cool. If any crystals were going to precipitate, they would do so by the time she returned from dinner.

Bronwen approached the barnlike Dining Commons with mingled excitement and nausea, always. Since Eric had graduated two years ago she had never really found a congenial table, and most of the time she bicycled home to share macaroni and cheese or baked red snapper with her roommate in their off-campus apartment, an attic converted by a retired butcher and his wife. One of its main virtues was its proximity to a new hamburger place called McDonald's, where you could get burgers for twenty-nine cents and salty shoestring fries for eleven.

There were many days when she was one of the three or four unable to bear another moment in the library, one of those who would arrive early at the dining hall and sit at the bare tables until the line opened at 4:30. Then she would eat slowly, staying on past 6:30, and feel so disgusted with herself that the evening was ruined. After another hour back in the library there would be a pilgrimage to the coffeeshop with the other haunted souls who could neither study nor enjoy themselves, but sat staring bleakly into unwanted cups of watery cocoa.

This evening, however, she approached her dinner with a faint sense of having hope. She wanted to prolong the feeling as long as possible. She slid her tray along, picking up pork steak with runny tomato sauce, spinach, pale yellow disks of carrots, egg custard and coffee that smelled like one of her organic lab assignments.

Pausing by the silverware she tried to decide where to sit, while fumbling with the napkins so it wouldn't be too obvious that she was terrified of this moment, of not seeming to know where she was welcome. In the center of this room, which contained about a hundred brown plastic-topped tables, was one around which twelve people were already clustered. It was meant to seat six. Three members of the group were old cronies from Eric's pseudo outlaw-biker days (so tough their license plates had read, "Born To Be Phi Bates"). Eric's best friend Peter had graduated years ago, but, unable to enter the real world, still hung around mooching food from other students at mealtimes, while otherwise occupying himself by reading Jung out loud in the coffeeshop to long-haired freshmen girls or improvising on a piano in the campus music building.

"Aha! It's the Queen of Acetone Alley! How goes it? Been workin' hard, McCuddhy? Smells like a dry cleaners, doesn't she? Whoo-ee! Talked to Eric lately? Is he bangin' anyone of note in Cambridge these days? Now that you're no longer available, of course ...." Gunter's whole body wriggled gleefully.

"I don't know," she said, bitterly regretting her decision to sit with them. She unzipped her jacket and hung it over the back of her seat. The paperback Rilke she propped open at random against a napkin dispenser.

"Hey, McCuddhy, what do you really think of Jung? Or, for that matter, what do you think of Peter? Hey, wow, look at her, she's wearing lipstick tonight. That must be for you, Peter!"

She stared steadily at her pork steak, concentrating on raising and lowering her fork. Peter really was extremely attractive, in a raunchy James Deansian sort of way. She couldn't take his World Traveler & Cynic posture very seriously, though, but was incapable of telling him so. He looked so unhappy most of the time. Eric had completely cut off their friendship when Peter's lack of academic ambition became all too apparent.

As she began on the custard, trying to include a little piece of the nutmeg-sprinkled crust with every spoonful, something on the page came into focus. It was from a letter Rilke had written in May 1904:

"There are so many things about which some old man ought to tell one while one is little; for when one is grown one would know them as a matter of course. There are the starry skies, and I do not know what mankind has already learned about them, not even the order of the stars do I know.

And so it is with flowers, with animals, with the simplest laws, that function here and there and go through the world in a few strides from beginning to end. How life occurs, how it operates in ordinary animals, how it ramifies and spreads, how life blossoms, how it bears: All that I long to learn. Through participation in it to bind myself more firmly to reality—which so often denies me—To Be Of It, not only in feeling but in knowledge, always and always; that I believe is what I need, to become more sure and not so homeless. You sense that I do not want sciences; for each one requires a lifetime and no life is long enough to master even its beginnings; but I want to cease to be an exile...."

"BRONWEN!! Peter's talking to you!" Gunter moved the napkin holder and the book fell over.

"What...what?" She fell unpleasantly back to earth.

"Listen, Bronwen," Peter began nervously, as if someone had put him up to it, "some guy in Berkeley told me about this anesthetic jelly, you know the kind you put on mosquito bites and cuts? That really numbs the nerves? Well, he says if you rub it on a guy's prick he can go for HOURS, man, and when you come—whooee! Don't you think Eric would be interested?"

Everyone at the table was staring at her.

"I don't know," she said for the second time, gulped down the remains of her cold, vile coffee and got up to return her tray.

"McCuddhy! What's the matter," Peter shouted at her retreating back, "you a prude or something?"

"She needs it *bad*," Gunter was confiding to someone as she passed their table on her way out. Aware that they were all watching her, she walked as stiffassedly as possible into the chilly September evening.

She headed towards the science complex to take a peep at her flask before heading home. At least it wasn't raining. Numbly she trudged across the vast green lawn. There was a soft murmur of voices from couples locked together in the secret caves the shrubbery made along the borders near the footpaths.

... to be of it. Not to be an exile. Felix and Caleb and Eric were all 3,000 miles away. And her father was dead. He never did make it to Tahiti. But that wasn't *her* fault. *It really wasn't her friggin' fault.* And she broke into a run, crushing fallen leaves and twigs beneath her boots as she flew down the path towards the lab.

The chemistry building was still and empty. On her lab bench something gleamed faintly in the gloom. Holding the flask up to the last weak sunlight filtering through the high, dusty windows, she saw clusters of pale green fluorescent crystals. They were clumped together in tiny multi-layered discs, resembling flakes of some exotic mica. She gave the flask a gentle shake, and more crystals materialized, pearly apple green, suspended in the grayish liquid but shining through it, like miner's lamps, like fireflies, like cat's eyes!

The crystals glowed in the dim light. Bronwen twirled the beaker, and again a shower of thin green flakes, new ones, descended through the chilled solvent.

All the way home, while her unlit bicycle coasted down the hill in the growing darkness, the shining flakes fell, again and again, filling her heart with a clear, cold light.

Barbara Riddle

Barbara Riddle was born in New York City and educated at Reed College and Brandeis University. She divides her time between Manhattan and St. Petersburg, Florida. This is her first novel.

Made in the USA
Las Vegas, NV
15 April 2022

47512418R00125